This is a work of Fiction.
although based in historical
the story it is a coincidence.

MW01126332

Credits

Thanks to: My wife who is so supportive and believed in me. Last my dogs who watch me act out the fight scenes and must wonder what the hell has gotten into their boss. Lastly thanks to those who sent me feedback for typos and errors.

The Dorset Boy Series Timeline

1792 – 1795   Book 1: A Talent for Trouble
Marty joins the Navy as an Assistant Steward and ends up a midshipman.

1795 – 1798   Book 2: The Special Operations Flotilla
Marty is a founder member of the Special Operations Flotilla, learns to be a spy and passes as lieutenant.

1799 – 1802   Book 3: Agent Provocateur
Marty teams up with Linette to infiltrate Paris, marries Caroline, becomes a father and fights pirates in Madagascar.

1802 – 1804   Book 4: In Dangerous Company
Marty and Caroline are in India helping out Arthur Wellesley, combating French efforts to disrupt the East India Company and French sponsored pirates on Reunion. James Stockley born

1804 – 1805   Book 5: The Tempest
Piracy in the Caribbean, French interference, Spanish gold and the death of Nelson. Marty makes Captain.

1806 – 1807   Book 6: Vendetta
A favour carried out for a prince, a new ship, the S.O.F. move to Gibraltar, the battle of Maida, counter espionage in Malta and a Vendetta declared and closed.

1807 – 1809   Book 7: The Trojan Horse
Rescue of the Portuguese royal family, Battle of the Basque Roads with Thomas Cochrane, and back to the Indian Ocean and another conflict with the French Intelligence Service.

1809 – 1811   Book 8: La Licorne
Marty takes on the role of Viscount Wellington's Head of Intelligence. Battle of The Lines of Torres Vedras, siege of Cadiz, skullduggery, espionage and blowing stuff up to confound the French.

1812   Book 9: Raider

Marty is busy. From London to Paris to America and back to the Mediterranean for the battle of Salamanca. A mission to the Adriatic reveals a white slavery racket that results in a private mission to the Caribbean to rescue his children.

1813-1814   Book 10: Silverthorn

Promoted to Commodore and given a Viscountcy Marty is sent to the Caribbean to be Governor of Aruba which provides the cover story he needs to fight American privateers and undermine the Spanish in South America. On his return he escorts Napoleon into Exile on Alba.

1815-1816   Book 11: Exile

After 100 days in exile Napoleon returns to France and Marty tries to hunt him down. After the battle of Waterloo Marty again escorts him into Exile on St Helena. His help is requested by the Governor of Ceylon against the rebels n Kandy.

Contents

Chapter 1: Leaving Home

"You're early again," said Miss Kate, the teacher at the school in Stoborough.

It was a long walk for a twelve-year-old from Furzebrook to Stoborough through the heath, which was yellow with gorse flowers at the end of June. Marty had started at just before dawn to get there at that time.

"I wanted time to look at the map Miss," he replied, but she knew that already. Marty was very bright, could read and write, do his numbers, and was absolutely fascinated by the "Map of the Known World" that he had discovered amongst the books at the back of the one room school, which was attached to the local Wesleyan chapel.

Katy Turner was a spinster in her forties and the local lay preacher. The church only existed because she was independently wealthy. The inheritor of her aunt's fortune which she used for good works. Her only relative was her younger brother, a Captain in the Royal Navy who was currently at sea. The school was how she tried to help the young of the parish to better themselves, but it was a hard job as most boys went into either mining or agriculture and the girls went into service at an early age. It was a simple, one room building with half a dozen tables, benches, and a large blackboard at one end. At this time of day, there was a pile of around ten slates in the corner and a bowl of chalks. When the children arrived, they would each be taught at their individual level in the same room. It helped that the oldest was only twelve.

She studied young Marty as he poured over the maps and, not for the first time, noted that he was thin and undersized for his age. That was what came from being the youngest of nine in a clay miner's family.

Clay mining was one of the only employers in the Isle of Purbeck where they mined the much sought-after ball clay that was used in everything from medicine to fine porcelain pottery. It was dug mainly in underground mines rather than opencast pits, and his father and brothers all worked in the Furzebrook mines as diggers.

His father wanted to get promoted to a cutter so he could work above ground at the Ridge weathering grounds, work that was less dangerous and strenuous. Ball clay was weathered for over a year before cutting and loading into carts to be taken down to the River Frome, where it was loaded onto barges that took it to the potteries in the midlands.

There was also work at the stone quarries on the other side of Corfe Castle. Some were opencast, but others were cut deep into the cliffs along the coast to get to the best stone that was sent to London and other big cities for their grand buildings.

At twelve years old, Marty would soon be heading down the pits himself. *What a waste,* she thought, *he has a good mind, and he isn't strong enough for that kind of work.* Miners dug the clay with picks and shovels in unventilated shafts deep in the ground lit only by a candle. The air was refreshed by throwing buckets of water down the shafts to drive the old air up and out. It was extremely hard and very dangerous as evidenced by the number of broken and crippled men who were only supported by their extended families having been discarded as useless by the mine owners.

Three weeks later, Marty didn't show up for school.

A week after that, she saw him as she rode her Landau Carriage down Furzebrook road from Creech where she had been visiting the Lady of the Manor. Trudging along with his brothers, caked head to foot in grey clay, looking thoroughly exhausted after a ten-hour shift down the pit. The boy looked wretched, and her heart went out to him, but what could she do?

When she got home, she found a letter from her brother. He had been in Plymouth when he wrote it. He told her he was back in England for resupply and would stop in at Poole so he could see her before heading back out to sea for another cruise.

Such is the power of a Navy Captain, she thought, *two hundred men and a frigate and he can just decide to stop off at Poole to see me*. But then a ghost of an idea started to form at the back of her mind – what if?

The next week went by slowly until finally the servant girl, Emily, came into her drawing room to announce that Captain James' carriage had arrived, and he was coming up the path to the house.

Nervously, she prepared herself to greet him, wondering if her idea would work or be dismissed out of hand. Her brother, even though the younger, always had a compelling and strong presence that she felt dominated by. Maybe it was the fact he was used to command and being obeyed. Not that he ever commanded her, but she felt it all the same.

He had long, dark hair worn in a Navy style queue tied with a black ribbon. Broad shouldered, his uniform looked good on his five-foot ten frame and his brown eyes were dark and focused on anyone he talked to with a fierce intensity. As a young man, he had been a fanatical rider of the hunt. That thrill of the chase was what made him a successful frigate captain.

She knew he had several women in his life, not that he was a womaniser but since his wife died, childless from fever, he had seemed to make a point of not getting involved with any single one. It helped that, as a sailor, he could keep them apart in separate cities and even countries.

As he entered the room, his face broke into a smile that transformed his normally stern, yet handsome face into the one she remembered as a boy. She rose to kiss him on the cheek and hug him fondly.

"My dear Katy. How are you? You are looking well."

"I am fine. Have you put on a little weight? That waistcoat looks like it could do with letting out a bit," she teased.

"Not at all! It's all the fashion. Tight breeches and tighter waistcoats you know," he laughed and gave a her another hug.

"How long are you here for?"

"Oh, I can stay a week. We picked up some damage during the storm two days ago, and it will give the crew time to make repairs. Poole is sheltered enough to do them safely, and we can get what we need there. My First is very capable and I can leave it all to him. We are also undermanned, lost a few through sickness and accidents and another dozen during a clash with a French privateer, so the recruiters will be out looking for replacements."

It was 1793 and the English were at war with the French again.

"You mean the press." She said with a grimace. "It is a horrible way to get men for the navy. It's just another form of slavery."

"Well yes, that too if I have to, but I will send men out to look for volunteers. I would rather have five volunteers than ten pressed men," he replied with a frown. "And I lost my cabin boy too. He was killed when he was hit by an eight pounder from that damn Frenchie. He didn't know anything about it, poor mite. Damn nuisance, he was just getting to be useful."

Oh my God, you move in mysterious and wonderful ways, she thought as her idea blossomed into a real possibility. "My dear, by an absolute coincidence, I may be able to solve that problem for you."

The next morning, she sent a messenger to the house of young Marty Stockley saying that she would be visiting with her brother later that day and would appreciate a meeting with his parents, Wilfred and Annie. She didn't say why.

In the evening, they took the landau and drove to the small estate cottage where the Stockley's lived. It was basically a mud and wattle two roomed building with a thatched roof where the whole family lived and apparently thrived, which was testament to the hardiness of the local people.

The door opened as they dismounted, and Wilfred and Annie came and stood outside the door looking concerned that they had attracted the attention of such esteemed visitors. Wilfred held his flat cap in his fists wringing the life out of it. Like many men in his line of work, he was older than his years, broken by the grinding labour. The children could be seen peering through the door from inside. The oldest boy, still at home at seventeen years old, stood boldly in the doorway trying to look grown up, with the rest of the children behind him. His two older brothers had left and got married when they were eighteen.

"We want to talk to you about Marty," Katie said.

"If 'e's caused trouble I'll 'ave is hide," growled Wilfred, "tha li'le bugger is allus up to somit."

"Wilf! Mind yer language in front of Miss Turner will yer," cried Annie, "Oh my! I'm so sorry, miss and sor. Whatever mus' youse think o' 'im."

Will the Dorset dialect ever acquire H's and T's, thought Katie, but instead she said, "Do not worry my dear, let me introduce my brother, Captain James Turner. It's because of him that we are here. You see, he is the Captain of His Majesties Frigate Falcon, and has recently become in need of a new cabin boy. I thought that your young Marty would fit the bill very nicely." She thought it would be prudent not to mention why there was a vacancy.

"Oh my!" gasped Annie, "but 'e be so little and..."

"Don't fret so," interrupted her husband with a slightly avaricious gleam in his eye. "'e ain't no good in the pit cus 'e be too small. What be it worth to ye to take him on like, cus me an 'is muvver cain't let 'im go fer nuttin." It was quite common for poor working families to sell off 'excess' children, so Marty's father saw nothing wrong with asking for money.

"My dear, sir," said Captain James, inwardly wincing at the accent, "I will give you a kings sovereign for the boy if he comes with us right away, and I will sign him on as a ship's boy, so he will get his eight pounds a year pay and a share of the prize money. I can arrange for, say, half his pay to be sent to you when the ship comes into its home port until he reaches his majority, if that's what he wants. My sister tells me the boy has some education and we will see that continues. So, if he proves proficient and able, he may progress in the Navy as any man can."

All Wilf heard was "I will give you a Kings sovereign now" and "eight pounds a year." The rest faded into the background as he thought of all the things he could buy with a whole sovereign! Beer mainly, but also extra food for the family! It was more than he earned in a month!

With almost indecent speed, young Marty was loaded into the Landau with his pathetically small pack of personal possessions, and they left to return to Katy's house. The cries of farewell from his mother and siblings rang in his ears but his father was fixated on the Sovereign that Captain Taylor had given him.

He now belonged to the Navy.

Chapter 2: The Adventure Begins

Marty was a little confused. Mainly because nobody had told him why he was being taken to Miss Taylor's big house, or why he was carrying all his worldly goods in a knotted cloth. He just knew that his mother had rubbed him down with a wet rag (as close to a wash as he ever got except when he swam in the river) and rushed him out of the house and into the carriage with all his siblings either yelling goodbye or crying their eyes out. He had been too far away from the door to hear anything that had been said, his brother had just smirked and said he was a jammy bugger as he patted him on the back.

He got an even bigger shock when Miss Turner said he had to be bathed – whatever that meant - and to his horror, found out in short order when the gardener, old Ted, literally tore his clothes off him and dunked him in a big tub of lukewarm water. Ted proceeded to gleefully scrub him with a brush and sponge and something that smelled awful (carbolic soap) which dislodged the lice and fleas all peasants carried around with them. He was dressed in new clothes, the like of which he had never seen before but were in fact old clothes from Captain Taylor left over from when he was a child. They were a bit big and very loose, but he hadn't ever felt anything that soft against his skin in all his life!

He was given a bedroom all to himself, that was both awesome and very scary as he had never been truly alone before. The bed was, to him, huge and incredibly soft; the mattress being stuffed with wool rather than straw. In reality it was just a small room in the servant's quarters. His first night's sleep was poor as he had never slept on his own before, and he cried a little bit because he missed his mum and brothers and sisters.

The biggest surprise was dinner in the kitchen with the cook, Mrs. Thatcher, and maid of all works, Emily. He had never seen so much food in all his life! He couldn't believe it and stuffed himself until he couldn't eat anymore. The rich beef stew and dumplings and steamed treacle pudding were just out of this world.

The toilet was still outside, though, but there was a seat not just a bucket and he had a chamber pot under his bed. (After all that rich food he needed them!). It was a different world. He was put to bed at 09:00 and roused again at 06:00. Emily told him he had to learn how to wait on the captain and he was going to have to learn quick as they were leaving in three days' time to join his ship in Poole.

Poole!! He had heard of that place. One of the kids at school had boasted they had been there, but he doubted he actually had. He knew that the next big town to Stoborough was Wareham as he had walked across the causeway and sat on the wharf by the river where small cargo ships tied up to unload. He had liked to sit and look at them and imagine that they come from some of the countries on the map. But Poole was all the way down to the end of the river where it met the sea. That was a world away even beyond where the clay barges tied up.

So, for three days, he carried trays, cleaned silver and brass, and did his three hours of schooling a day. He learnt how you cleaned shoes and boots and that the captain wanted his shining so you could see your face in them. He learnt how to brush a coat. He tried to learn how to strop a razor but that was beyond him. He burned his fingers, stubbed his toes, and even managed to give himself a bloody nose pulling a strap off a sea trunk. It gave way in a rush and his own hand punched him in the face, but he didn't cry again as he had told himself this was a good thing, and his Mum needed to be proud of him.

After three days, the captain had his trunk and little Marty loaded on to a carriage. Marty sat on top with the driver in the open, not inside with the captain, but it didn't matter as it was a beautiful summer day and the weather was warm and dry. They bid farewell to Katy, who made him promise to write to her and tell of his adventures, and not to forget to write to his family.

With a shake of the reins, the driver got the horses moving, and they set off on the short journey to Wareham where the captain said his barge would be waiting to take them down river to the docks at Poole. For Marty, though, this was epic; the view from the high carriage was like nothing he had ever seen. He could even see all the way down the river to Redcliff as they passed over the bridge into Wareham.

He could see ships tied up at the wharf and labourers unloading them, carrying sacks and bales of unidentified stuff to carts which would carry them to warehouses. He also saw a smart Navy barge painted dark blue with a white stripe. The crew, who had been lounging, sat straight and held the oars upright when someone spotted the coach approaching. The sailors were all dressed in matching blue and white striped shirts, black straw hats and white trousers. There was a man dressed a bit like the captain who looked to be in charge and as they got closer, he realized it wasn't a man at all but a boy of around sixteen years old.

As old Tom had told him before the start of the trip, he jumped down first and pulled down the metal steps for the captain to make an elegant exit from the coach. He stayed behind the captain, who was met by one of the sailors who touched his forelock as he approached the boat.

The young man in uniform saluted the captain and greeted him politely, in what Marty assumed was an aristocratic voice. The captain asked if all was well and was told that they had a new intake of eight volunteers and ten pressed men, two of which came from the magistrate. Gaol sweepings, men who had committed a petty crime or had got in to debt and had opted for sea service rather than a term in gaol.

All repairs had been done, replenishing completed, and the ship was in all respects ready for sea. Marty wondered if their ship was as big as some of the ships tied up against Wareham wharf!

The midshipman then told Marty to get into the barge and muttered that the captain was always last in and first out, so to look lively and get himself boarded! The captain's trunk followed with the duffel bag of things that Miss Taylor had given him and, finally, the great man himself.

The midshipman stood at the back of the boat and steered using a long pole thing and the sailors all pulled on their sticks together at the command 'Give way together!' Marty had seen boats on the river before, but he had never been in one and he had never even talked to a boatman. So, it wasn't much of a surprise that he felt a little queasy as the barge gently rolled.

The barge moved with frightening speed, faster than the coach had. Of course, he had no idea that they were going downstream, and the barge had to travel faster than the water to maintain steerage. At that time, the river was in spate as there had been a large amount of rain upstream the day before, so they were flying along. He saw the red cliffs approaching and saw his brother, Alfred, and his sisters, Helen and Jane, standing on the beach waving furiously. Miss Turner must have told them he would be passing today. They would have gotten a ride down on one of the clay carts to Ridge. He waved back to them and then caught a look from the sailor next to him who rolled his eyes towards the back of the boat where the captain sat. A quick glance showed him that the captain was pointedly looking the other way and the other officer was focusing downstream. So, he figured he had got away with whatever crime he had committed.

It wasn't long before the river widened out below Ridge into the estuary and the Arne peninsula, with its extensive reed beds and rich birdlife. He spotted a water fowler in a punt with a long gun mounted at the front. He was using two short oars to manoeuvre the punt into line with a large flock of waterfowl. There was a huge cloud of smoke from the muzzle and a loud bang and a number of birds dropped into the water. The captain said something to the midshipman, who steered the barge towards the punt and hailed the man.

The wildfowler introduced himself as Arthur Coombes and after a brief exchange, six birds were secured, and coins changed hands. Well, even the captain had to eat, Marty supposed, and six birds would feed everyone on the boat.

The trip continued on, the crew raised a mast and set a sail as they came out into the estuary proper. The mood in the boat became cheerful as the men relaxed and enjoyed the ride with very little to do except trim the sail at the barked orders of the midshipman.

The wind seemed to drop but the boat didn't slow down. Marty finally figured it out; the wind was almost coming from behind them and blowing them along, and they were travelling at almost the same speed as it was. So it felt like it was less than it was when they were going slower. He was proud of figuring that out on his own.

After a while, they turned around the hook of Arne towards the East and the South-westerly wind that had been on their backs now came around to the right side of the barge. He was surprised as they speeded up. That was odd. He didn't understand that at all; surely, they should slow down if the wind wasn't behind them. He would have to ask about that at some point.

But soon the entrance to Poole Harbour came into view and he could see that there were three masts that stood way above all the others. As they came up with Brownsea Island on their right, the ship they belonged to came slowly into view. To his eyes, she was huge, masts towering into the sky, her gun ports open looking like a row of windows. He counted fourteen on the side he could see.

There were men scrambling around by a gap in the side at the top of the hull. Some were dressed like soldiers with red coats and white belts and held muskets. He had seen soldiers marching around with a drummer trying to get men to join the Dorsetshire foot regiment in the village. The rest were dressed in blue uniform coats and black hats.

There was a shout of, "Boat Ahoy," and one of the men in the boat called back, "Falcon."

That's daft, he thought, because anybody could see that the barge was the captain's, and he was sitting in plain view in the back.

As the boat pulled up to the side, the man at the front stood up with a pole with a hook on the end and latched it on to the chains hanging from the side. The men raised the oars closest to the ship and the oars on the other side were used to work the boat tight up against the side. One of the men at the back tossed a rope up to a sailor at the rail of the ship securing it.

The captain stood, placed his hat firmly on his head, shifted his sword so it was clear of his legs, and started to climb up the side. There were wooden battens fixed to the side of the ship to form a sort of ladder and ropes hung down from either side, held out by young boys, that could be used to help the climber.

That shouldn't be any harder than climbing a tree, Marty thought.

As the captain's head rose above the deck, there was a squeal of whistles and a crash of boots stamping on the deck. He noticed a small cloud of white dust rise above the soldiers. It was all very odd. Once the captain was on board, had talked to the men greeting him and moved away, the other officer in the boat started up the side.

"Stay where you are," growled a fierce looking man who had been sitting in the back next to the captain who then surprised Marty by smiling at him. "So, you are the new cabin boy, are you? What's your name?"

"Marty, Sur"

"Don't call me Sir. I ain't no officer. I'm the cap'n's coxswain, so just call me Cox. You just sit tight there for now and once we have swayed up the cap'n's trunk you can get a free ride up to the deck when they haul up the barge. Just stay in the middle there out of the way."

"Yes, Cox," said Marty

"In the Navy its Aye Aye, not yes. Try it out."

"Aye Aye, Cox."

"That's a good lad. Now, do as I said."

Marty stayed put as the trunk was passed up the side by a couple of burly sailors and then ropes were lowered and attached to the barge from a boom that stuck out over the side of the ship. A tune started up on a fiddle and suddenly the barge started to rise. He noticed there was only himself and two sailors left, and they looked at him with big grins on their faces.

Up rose the barge over the rail then swung in to the centre of the ship where it was lowered onto a cradle.

"Out you get, young un," said a big man with tattoos on his arms, a noticeable broken nose, and piercing blue eyes.

Marty jumped over the side and clambered down onto the deck. He was astonished by the number of men working around him. He didn't know it, but the Falcon had a complement of two hundred men when she was fully up to strength but like many Navy ships, she was shorthanded. It looked chaotic, but each man knew his station or was being educated the hard way with bosun's mates urging them to the right place with blows from rattan starters.

The cox appeared beside him and said,

"Come on, son. I'll take you down to your quarters."

Marty followed and heard him greet several men on the way, one called him John in return to his "hello Frank, meet up for a wet later?" He filed that information away for later as it was obvious that John the cox was a respected member of the crew.

On the way, they were stopped by a tall man in uniform who the cox introduced as the First Lieutenant. He peered down at Marty and said,

"The runt of the litter Cox?"

"Yes, he is a small one alright, but the Cap'n thinks he'll soon fill out with decent food," he replied, "he can read and write, apparently, which is an improvement on the last one."

"Well, get him signed on to the books then settle him in below. We are getting underway directly before we lose the tide," the Lieutenant said as he moved away towards the raised deck at the back of the ship.

The cox nodded towards the raised deck and said,

"That be the quarterdeck and only the officers of the watch and the Cap'n be allowed up there. So, don't go wandering up there without permission. Now, we need to see the Purser to get you signed on."

He led the way to a stair that they took down into the hull and then down another to what the cox called the Orlop. The Purser was found in a small room which was part bedroom and part office. He was a fat, little man called Mr. Evans with a shrewd face and an accent that Marty didn't recognise. It was sort of singsong, and he pronounced 'right' as 'royt'. He entered Marty's name in a big book where all the crew were listed and put a V next to it. That was because he was a volunteer, he said. He asked Marty's age and birth date and entered it with today's date in a separate column. Last, he bade him sign his name. Marty did and noticed that many of the sailors had just put an X by theirs. He also noticed he was given the title of "Ship's Boy."

He gave him some clothes, or slops, as he called them, a bowl, a mug, and a knife and was told to sign in yet another book for them.

"If you want or need anything else, you can ask me for it, and it will be taken out of your pay."

That was news, he didn't know he would get paid for this.

That done, the cox took him and his load back up on deck then aft to a set of stairs that led down in front of the quarterdeck. At the bottom stood a soldier who guarded a door to the captain's cabin. When he asked about him, the cox laughed and said that the 'soldiers' were in fact marines, and he had better not make that mistake again in earshot of any of them if he didn't want a beating. Near to the captain's door was another, shielded by a curtain, which they pushed through to find a small wiry man, who the cox introduced as the cap'n's steward, Esidiah Isaacs. Esi, as he said to call him, had a prominent nose and an accent that was later identified as coming from Northeast London. He had joined the Navy after being caught defrauding the tailor he worked for and chosen the Navy over prison.

Esi showed Marty his berth, which was at one end of the gun deck with the other boys. A berth amounted to a hammock and a sea chest. Esi told him to change into his slops and to stow his good clothes in his chest. When Marty asked where the toilet was as he needed to go, he was told he had to use the heads. Taking in his confused look, Esi led him to the bow of the ship and showed him the platform with holes in where he could sit and relieve himself over the sea. By now, the ship was under sail passing around Brownsea Island to head towards Studland and the open sea and even though the sea was calm in the sheltered bay, the thought of hanging over the water stopped him dead.

"Keep one hand for the boat and one fer yerself," a crewman said as he hoisted himself out with his trousers around his knees. So, grabbing his courage, he held on for grim death with one hand and managed to complete the task with the other.

Back at the steward's quarters, Esi handed him a tray with a coffee pot, cream jug, sugar, cup, and saucer. "Take that in to the captain. He wants to see you, so you just as well make yourself useful."

Remembering what he had been taught in the last week, he made his way through the connecting door into the captain's day room. Just at that point, the ship came out from behind Studland and through the gap into the Channel. She gave a stutter and a bit of a buck as her bow hit the first of the swell, and Marty staggered forward just catching his balance before he deposited the coffee on to the captain's lap!

The captain's eye's widened for a split second, and he recovered his poise with a visible effort when he saw the danger pass.

"You need to get your sea legs," he said.

"Aye Aye, sir," Marty replied, even though he had no idea what "sea legs" were.

Once he had safely deposited the tray on the desk, the captain addressed him.

"Well, Martin Stockley, you are now a member of his Majesty's Navy. You are, in fact, my junior servant but we have signed you on as a ship's boy so you can learn the ship and have the chance to become a useful crewman in the future. As well as your duties here in my quarters, you will be allocated a Sea Daddy who will teach you the ropes. My sister says you have a fair hand at writing, so you will also assist my clerk, Mr. Waldcotter, as needed. You will attend classes with the Gunner's wife and continue to improve your reading, writing, and arithmetic. You are expected to keep yourself clean and obey the rules of the ship. Do you understand?"

"Aye Aye, sir," said Marty enthusiastically but with a slight feeling of trepidation.

"Good, now get along. My cox will show you around the ship and introduce you to your sea daddy."

Back in the steward's galley, he approached Esi, who was busy polishing a silver dinner set with brick dust.

"Esi, what's a sea daddy?"

Esi laughed and said,

"So, you are getting one, are you? Well, a sea daddy is an older sailor who takes on a youngster and teaches him all the things that a sailor needs to know. Do you know who?"

At that moment, the cox stuck his head through the curtain and said,

"He's being put with Tom Savage. He's a good man and steady."

"Aye, he is that," agreed Esi.

"Come on young'un, it be time for you to see around your new home," said the cox as he turned to lead him out.

Marty didn't know it, but this was not the normal introduction of a boy into ship's life, but the captain was under strict orders from his sister and was sure that she would ask the boy for an account of all his new adventures when she wrote to him.

For the next hour or so, they went around the ship with the cox naming all the main parts. He learnt which were the Mizzen, Main, and foremasts and what a bowsprit and figurehead were. The Falcon's figure head was a fierce depiction of a falcon swooping with its talons outstretched and its beak wide as if it were screaming defiance at the world. It was very impressive, and he was told the captain had commissioned it himself.

He was shown where he could walk without getting in anyone's way, and then they went down to the Gun Deck where the main armament of nine-pound cannon were. It was dark and stuffy down there and smelt terrible,

"That's the smell of sweat, farts, and bilges," Cox told him with a laugh. He was shown where the ward room and midshipmen's cockpit were, and visited the Orlop deck where he was introduced to the surgeon, who smelt of brandy, and the purser who he had already met. He was shown where the bread room was and where to find the captain's private supplies.

He was introduced to the Gunner's wife, the only woman on the ship, Mrs. Crumb, a plump matronly woman who had a shrewd eye and gave him a thorough once over.

"Can you read and do yer numbers?" she asked.

"Aye aye, miss," he said.

She laughed. "You don't need to say aye, aye to me. A simple yes will do. Who taught you?"

"Miss Turner, miss," he said.

"What, the Cap'n's sister? Oh my," she said, "I'd heard she was teaching but didn't think it was true. Well, I have a lot to live up to then. You be here at two bells of the day watch tomorrow and we will have three hours of lessons."

They found Tom Savage on the main deck splicing two ropes together. He was the same man he had seen when he climbed out of the barge.

"Come to me when I'm off watch and oi'l show you the ropes, young'un," the old salt growled.

Lastly, he was taken to the captain's clerk's cabin and introduced to Mr. Waldcotter. A slight man of middle years with ink-stained fingers who looked slightly aggrieved at having a youngster thrust on him as an assistant. He made Marty copy a short note he had on his desk and was surprised when he was presented with a neat copperplate copy with no mistakes.

Back in the steward's galley, Marty sat on a box and thought about all he had seen and been told. It was all jumbled in his head right then and the amount he had to learn looked like a mountain. For a long minute, he felt panic creeping up on him. But then he remembered something Miss Katy always said – When a problem looks like a mountain, look for the rocks that you can fix one at a time.

This ship is just too big to get all at once, he thought, *I just need to go step by step.* And then a new determination came on him and he knew he could do it.

Chapter 3: Settling In

Life settled down to the rhythm of life at sea for the next couple of weeks. Up before dawn to serve the captain his breakfast, down to his lessons with Mistress Crumb, back to the captain's stewards galley to polish, clean, press or wash whatever needed polishing, cleaning, pressing or washing, check with the clerk if anything needed copying, then out on deck to find Tom to learn his knots, how to splice, what all the ropes in the rigging meant and how to climb the masts safely.

But all work and no play made Marty a dull boy and there were other children on the Falcon. The ship's boys were mostly younger than him but there were a couple who were around the same age and who he could play with. All of them were general dog's bodies during the everyday running of the ship. Some acted as 'nippers', who used short lengths of rope to 'nip' the anchor hawse to the endless messenger rope around the capstan so the anchor could be hauled, or heavy loads lifted. Others were powder monkeys who brought up the cartridges from the magazine to the guns in wooden cartridge holders. Something he witnessed during the first live fire practice he saw.

The other group of young men were midshipmen. These young gentlemen were officers in training, were the most junior officers on board, and had responsibility of between thirty and fifty men each in the ship's divisions. There were five mids in total, the youngest of which was the same age as Marty, and were led by the Senior midshipman, Mr. Fairbrother. He was twenty-one years old, had passed his lieutenant's exams, but was, like many mids, waiting for an opportunity to advance. He knew it was just a matter of time as Captain Taylor had a reputation for spotting and training good officers.

In his down time, Marty started to get to know and make friends with the ship's boys. The only problem was that the oldest of them, a fourteen-year-old called Billy Smith, was a bully. He only picked on the youngest and smallest and that made Marty a natural target. But Marty was the seventh son of a miner and was well used to fighting his own corner. So, it was inevitable that there would be a reckoning, and after two weeks at sea on the Sunday 'Make and Mend' day, Marty and Billy faced off on the main deck. Billy had deliberately tripped Marty and knocked him to the deck, and Marty had shot to his feet, fists clenched, ready for battle. Sailors nearby who could witness what was going on just watched with interest as the two young cocks circled each other ready to 'get stuck in.'

Marty knew if he let the bigger boy win, his life would be misery. He also knew if he let him get in close, he would lose in short order, so he made sure he kept his distance and out of the grasp of the young bully. His hit and run tactics so frustrated the bigger boy that he gave a roar of frustration and charged to grapple Marty to the floor. Marty saw that coming and dropped to his hands and knees, tripping Billy so that he landed flat on his face and knocked the breath out of him. In a flash, Marty was up, jumped on his back, grabbed his hair and pounded his head on the deck. This caused Billy to yell in pain, which attracted the attention of one of the bosun's mates, who watched with amusement until he saw the First Lieutenant coming then moved in with one of the sailors to break it up. Marty was picked bodily off of Billy, and Billy was dragged to his feet by his hair and held in place.

Now, the First Lieutenant arrived on the scene, wondering what the fuss was about on a day that should have been calm and peaceful. One look told him all he needed to know. Two boys being separated by a bosun's mate and a crew man. One, the captain's cabin boy, and the other, the oldest ship's boy, who had blood pouring out of his nose, a cut on his forehead and the start of a pair of cracking black eyes. He suppressed a smile at the sight and instead put on his fiercest frown.

"You two! I will not have public displays of discord on my ship! I don't care what started it; although it's clear who won." That caused a laugh amongst the audience of crewmen. "You will both kiss the gunner's daughter and receive ten reminders why fighting isn't allowed on a King's Ship."

Five minutes later, howls of pain were heard accompanied by the swish-crack of a rattan cane striking young buttocks. Discipline had been re-established, and a tearful Marty slunk back to his berth to nurse his pride and lay on his front to preserve his tender behind. The upside was that Billy now studiously avoided him except when they were both at their lessons. Marty, on the other hand, gained an eager following of the younger boys and more mischief would inevitably follow.

Their destination, it seemed, was somewhere called Gibraltar, and he wished he had his map so he could see where that was. He eventually got the chance to ask the cox who was surprised that he was even interested.

"Let's go see the sailing master and see if he can show you." He offered.

Old Trubshaw, the sailing master, was one of the oldest men on the ship. He had close cropped grey hair and a full beard that Marty thought made him look as if his head had been put on upside down. He had just finished taking the noon sighting with the mids, who were wandering off to their various duties. Some with smiles on their faces as they had correctly or even closely established the noon position or with looks of consternation because they had put the ship closer to Norway than their actual position just off of Lisbon.

He smiled when the cox told him what they wanted and took them into the chart room where he unrolled a large chart which covered Spain, Portugal, and the coast of North Africa.

"This is where we are right now," he said, indicating a point about an inch off the coast of Lisbon.

"Down here where the gap between Spain and Africa is at its smallest are the straits of Gibraltar, and here on a peninsula off of the Spanish coast is Gibraltar. We will sail due South or a bit West of it until we get just South of the straits and then turn to run up through the straits with the wind on our stern."

"How do you know when to turn East?" Marty asked as you couldn't see anything but sea where Mr. Trubshaw had indicated they would make the turn.

"That, my boy, is a question of navigation. We measure our longitude against the sun at noon or known stars by means of a quadrant or one of these new sextants." He then picked up a polished wooden box and laid it on the table and when he opened it, there was a beautiful example of the instrument makers art. "When you are older, I will show you how to use it, but you need a lot more mathematics yet."

"What if there are clouds and you can't see the sky?" Marty asked, careful not to touch.

"Then we rely on dead reckoning," replied the master. "We know where we were the last time we got a good fix, we know how fast we travelled, the direction of any current, how long we travelled for, and the compass direction we travelled in. So, we can then plot where we think we should be." That gave Marty plenty to think about. It didn't sound easy at all.

Up to then, the weather had been unseasonably light. Even the notorious Bay of Biscay hadn't really given them any trouble, which was why it had taken two weeks to get down to Lisbon. However, the next morning Marty heard Mid Shipman Graveny tell the captain,

"The master's complements, sir. He says the sea is getting up and that there is a storm approaching from the Southwest."

"Tell him I will be on deck directly," replied the captain.

Two hours later, Marty felt like he wanted to die. The ship was pitching, rolling, and corkscrewing in the most horrible fashion as a full-blown Atlantic storm shrieked through the rigging and the ship and crew fought for their very lives. If the storm had blown in slower, they may have risked heading into one of the Portuguese ports, but it had hit them so fast that all they could do was put out a sea anchor, batten down the hatches, and hope to ride it out.

For thirty-six hours, he was thrown around in his cot incapable of doing more than groan and hang on. But eventually the wind started to die down and the ship's motion quieted, enabling Esi to put a cold plate together for the captain to have a light meal. Marty took it in and just as he placed it on the table, he heard a cry of, "SAIL HO!" from above followed by the sound of someone running down the quarterdeck stairs.

"Midshipman Wilson, Sah!" Bellowed the marine sentry. "Enter," said the captain.

The young mid (the same one who was in charge of the captain's barge) shot through the door and hauled up in front of the captain with an excited look on his face.

"Mr. Wilson," said the captain, "you appear to be somewhat exercised by something. So much so that you not only crashed into my cabin but seem to have forgotten to take off your hat."

Mr. Wilson looked horrified and started to stammer an apology and say that he brought the First Lieutenant's compliments.

"Mr. Wilson, your hat?" said the captain. Once he had removed it, the captain nodded and said, "Now what was it that Mr. Gentry would have you tell me?"

"Mr. Gentry's compliments, sir, but there is a strange sail to the Northeast, and they think it's maybe a Frenchie," he blurted out.

"Please inform the First Lieutenant that I will be up directly and to set a course to intercept."

"Aye Aye, SIR," said the mid and spun to leave.

"Mr. Wilson! In an orderly fashion if you please," said the captain, causing Wilson to halt in his tracks and resume at a more leisurely pace.

Once the door had closed, quietly, he looked up at Marty and said,

"The hunt is on! Fetch me my sword and pistols." Marty did as he was told, retrieving the blade from the rack and the Sharpe model 1760 pistols from the cupboard where they were kept. These brutally functional .55-inch calibre pistols were very different from the standard issue Sea Service Pistols issued to the men, which also doubled up as a club or a hammer once they had been fired.

The cox came in and said,

"Looks like a privateer, sir. Damaged rigging but still trying to make a run for it."

He took the pistols from Marty and carefully loaded and primed them, showing Marty each step. Then belted the captain's sword around his waist and clipped each of the pistols to the belt using the built-in belt hooks. Lastly he went to the wall behind the captain's desk and reached down a brass hunting horn slung with an ornate knotted rope and passed that to the captain.

"You stay with Esi on the Orlop deck during the fight," the cox told him as he and the captain made their way to the door.

"You don't know enough yet to be on deck, you will just get in the way."

The next twenty minutes saw him and Esi rushing around packing the tea sets and breakables into boxes that were specially made for the job. In another thirty minutes, they heard the command, "CLEAR FOR ACTION" being bellowed out by the First Lieutenant. Immediately, sailors appeared and started taking down the partition walls of the cabin, moving the furniture out and down into the hold for storage and clearing the area so the aft guns were ready for use. From call to action to readiness took just under twenty minutes. The Falcon was an efficient ship.

Chapter 4: The Hunt Is On!

Contrary to his expectations, nothing seemed to happen for the next half hour or so and his curiosity was getting the better of him. He could feel that the ship was travelling fast and hear the rush of water against the hull, but apart from shouted commands filtering down from above, he couldn't hear much else.

So, he decided to go take a look. Esi was snoozing, so he quietly left the Orlop deck, and climbed up to the main deck. On his way up, he was surprised to see Marine sentries standing at the top of each flight of stairs. He would find out later they were to stop men deserting their posts and hiding below decks when the fighting started.

The gun deck was completely cleared of all the hamper of tables and benches. The tables were slung up against the ceiling and the benches were stowed in the hold along with the sailors' personal belongings. The men were sat around their guns shirtless. Most with rags tied around their heads covering their ears. Ships boys were crouched along the centreline with their wooden cartridge boxes.

Up on the main deck, he got himself tucked in behind the ladder to the quarterdeck where he could see what was going on. Looking forward, he could see a ship ahead of them with all sails set running as if the devil itself were after them. She wasn't as big as the Falcon, and she looked like she was missing the top of her main mast and there was a big three-coloured flag streaming out behind. Above him, he could hear the captain and the first talking.

"We are almost in range of the bow chasers, sir," said the first.

"Try a shot at maximum range," said the captain. "Let's see if we can knock a spar off and slow him down."

After that, there was a boom and a cloud of noxious grey smoke drifted down the deck as the first bow chaser tried the range. There was no reaction from the crew, who were all looking toward the quarterdeck as if waiting for something to happen. The second bow chaser went off, and then he heard the captain cry, "Tally Ho! The hunt is on!" and then the shrill sound of his hunting horn sounding out the chase.

A great cheer went up from the men, and they all stood and got into position by their guns. The bow chasers fired again, and he heard the first say

"Oh, good shooting that took down his mizzen royal. We are catching him faster now."

"Load the Starboard battery, double shotted," the captain said. "And then get ready to turn two points to larboard." Commands were shouted, and the men went about servicing their guns. First, they were drawn back inboard, then a cartridge of powder was pushed into the barrel and seated home with a ram. Then, a wad of cotton, a ball, a wad, another ball, and a final wad all pressed down tight by the rammer. The gun captain pushed a long needle down through the touch hole, gave it a wiggle, and pulled it out. Finally, he poured fine gunpowder from a flask into the touch hole, stood back, and raised his arm.

"Run out!"

There was a rumble as the men hauled on the ropes to run the guns out, the gun captains ordered the men to train the pieces as far forward as they could go.

"Two points to larboard quartermaster."

"Fire as you bear. On the up roll."

The most forward gun fired first, followed by each gun in turn as the enemy crossed in front of the barrels. The noise was incredible, and the most exciting thing young Marty had ever seen or heard. Thick, grey, stinking, sulphurous smoke drifted back along the deck and when it cleared, he saw that the French chase had caught the majority of it across their larboard quarter. Her quarterdeck and mizzen were shot away, and she was wallowing in the breeze.

"Bring us alongside, serve her another broadside, and prepare to board," said the captain. "They haven't struck. See! Someone's putting their colours back up on the main."

Just as he said it, the side of the Frenchman lit up as she let loose her own broadside of the French equivalent of six-pound cannon, which although smaller than the Falcon's nine-pounders, still had a devastating hit at close range. Shot whistled by overhead and there were a couple of resounding crashes from forward. There was a scream from above and when he looked up, he saw a Marine falling directly at him. He was transfixed. Then, the poor man hit a stay that changed his direction of fall so that he landed across the barrel of the gun nearest to where Marty hid. There was a hideous crack as his back was broken and his screaming stopped as blood gushed out of his open mouth. Two of the gunners grabbed his body and just threw it out of the gun port.

A few seconds later and all the guns went off as one at almost point-blank range, and then the ship's hulls ground together and with a mighty roar the crew of the Falcon leapt across the gap with cutlasses, tomahawks and boarding pike glinting wickedly in the sun. There was an answering roar from the French ship and soon mayhem ruled.

He was about to leave his hiding place when two men landed on the deck in front of him. He knew instantly they were French; both had a sword and a pistol and were sneaking towards the stairs to the quarterdeck. He heard the captain's voice cheer his men on and saw both men raise their pistols ready to shoot.

Without thinking, he ran out of his hidey-hole, grabbed a rammer from the nearest gun, and screaming at the top of his voice, swung it at the backs of the Frenchmen as hard as he could. It didn't quite go to plan, but his rammer did connect with the man on the right just under his right arm, knocking him sideways into the other just as they both pulled their triggers. It was enough to spoil their aim and the shots went wide. The second man spun around and saw Marty standing there, rammer in hand, now feeling exposed and not quite knowing what to do next. Luckily, the captain, who was on his way to join the boarders, came to the bottom of the ladder and fired a pistol with his left hand almost directly into the face of the man Marty had hit. The ball burst the man's head like a melon spraying gore in all directions. He then thrust forward with his sword and skewered the second man through the side into his chest. He fell to the deck, pulling himself off the captain's blade and died with blood pouring from his mouth and nose.

"Get below!" he bellowed at Marty and then raised his hunting horn to his lips, blew the chase, and launched himself over the side into the mad fray on the other ship.

It all ended rather quickly after that. The Frenchman struck, the crew were disarmed, and the survivors held captive in the cable tier. Then, the crew of the Falcon set about making the two ships ready to be sailed to Gibraltar.

Marty and Esi made their way back to the captain's cabin and started to reinstall his things where they belonged once his cabin had been reconstructed. They had just about got halfway when the cox came in looking cross, came up to Marty, and said,

"I thought I told you to stay with Esi in the Orlop and keep out of trouble? But no, you had to sneak up on deck did'n you. Now, the captain wants to see you on the quarterdeck, so come along and be sharp about it. He's not to be kept waiting."

They emerged into the sunlight to the sound of hammers and saws. A quick look around showed him the French ship off their Starboard side with the British colours flying over the French on a jury-rigged mizzen mast.

A push in the back started him up the steps to the quarterdeck. He was frankly terrified; he had gotten ten stripes on his behind for fighting. How many would he get for disobeying the cox?

He was led to where the captain stood talking to the First Lieutenant and the sailing master and stood quietly waiting for his doom. They finished their conversation, and the captain turned and noticed him standing there next to the cox.

"Ahh gentlemen, we have the hero of the hour amongst us," he said.

Crickey, that must have been the cox Marty thought and was surprised when the captain rested his hand on his head and said

"If it wasn't for this young terrier, I would have a pair of French pistols shot in my chest. Felled two of them with a mighty swing of a ram, giving me the chance of finishing them off."

That's not quite right thought Marty but good sense kept his mouth shut. In any case, the whole episode was beginning to become a blur in his memory.

He looked around at the smiling faces of the men and just bobbed his head in acknowledgement.

"However, it seems he disobeyed my Cox who clearly told him to stay below and, even though we all know he is up for a fight, (more smiles and the odd titter from the men) has had no training in the arts of war."

Oh, here it comes, Marty thought *I'm going to be kissing the gunner's daughter again.*

"So, to teach him discipline and to give him the means to defend himself in the next scrape he gets into, he will attend weapons class with the rest of the crew."

Surprised, Marty just stood there with his mouth agape.

"Learn well your lessons in arms, young man, and now get along and get back to your duties."

That evening, when he finally got to his berth, he found himself the centre of attention amongst the other boys and found that he quite liked it. He had never had it before, and his ego swelled with every question and comment.

The next morning, though, he also got his first lesson in humility. Cox tipped him out of his hammock an hour before his regular time to get up and told him to, "follow me." He took him back down to the Orlop deck. Not to the place he was supposed to have stayed with Esi but further forward to the hospital space where the surgeon ruled. It was dark, lit only by lanthorns, men were laid out on cots, some asleep, but others groaned in agony from their wounds. They stopped by a man who he recognized as Tom a friend of the cox. His head was covered with a bandage that hid one side of his face and blood had seeped through it, staining it red.

"How is it Tom?" asked the cox as he put his hand on the other man's arm.

"Bad John, bad" he replied. "That damn Frenchie took my eye and opened up my face like a pumpkin," he said.

"The surgeon stitched you up ok, though," said the cox. "He tells me as long as it don't go rotten, you will be back on deck with the rest of us in a couple of weeks."

"Aye, if the stink rot don't set in," Tom replied. "but you know that's more likely than not," he paused, obviously gathering himself. "If'n it does," he said at last "finish me fast. I don't want to have it drag out like some of those other poor buggers who've gone before."

"Mate, you are going to be fine. But if the worst comes to the worst, I give you my word, you won't suffer," Cox John assured him.

After that, they came up on deck. The cox lent on the rail, looked out to sea, and took a deep breath.

"Would you really finish him?" asked Marty in a quiet voice.

The cox looked down at him and said, "War is an awful thing, boy, and on a ship, you fights for your mates, your ship, and your captain if you're lucky enough to get one like ours. Tom is like a brother to me and if that is what he wants, then I will do it, even though it breaks my heart. Dying from the stink rot is about the worst way a man can die, and I won't let him suffer like that. He just don't deserve it"

He turned back to look at the sea and just then the first light of morning brightened the morning sky and they could hear the ship coming to life.

Time to get to work, thought Marty. But he reached out and held the cox's hand briefly, giving it a squeeze before he left.

Chapter 5: Gibraltar

The next few days saw Marty start his education in weapons training. His arms ached from swinging a cutlass and thrusting with a boarding pike. He was paired up with the youngest midshipman, Simon Clegg, as they were of an age, and the two of them had at it enthusiastically with wooden practice swords in mock combat. This earned him a few choice bruises where Simon's sword made contact, but he felt he was giving as good as he got.

So, it was with a partial sense of relief that the two ships made the turn West in to the straits and made their way into the port of Gibraltar. Falcon's guns boomed out a salute to the Governor and Port Admiral as she turned smartly into the wind and dropped her anchor.

There was a lot of bustling and shouting as the men made sure the sails were neatly folded, harbour gaskets fitted, and lines flaked down. The master was rowed around the ship to see that all the yards were squared, and everything was ship shape. The prize was moored up a short way away, and a number of boats came out from the harbour with armed soldiers to take her over and to offload the French crew.

While all that was happening, Marty kept out of the way and listened to the chatter of the men, the scuttlebutt, as they called it. He learned that the prize was a French privateer and that she was not as well manned as you would normally expect because she had been successful and had a number of prize crews on captures. The prizes had been scattered by the storm, and no one knew if they had survived or not.

She did, however, have a choice cargo on board that had been taken from some of their prizes. The men expected her to be 'bought in' whatever that meant and that there would be prize money for all. As for the crew of the prize, they weren't French Navy, and wouldn't be exchanged for British sailors who had been captured by the French but would either spend time in gaol or just be released into Spain and have to make their own way back to wherever they came from.

The captain was rowed ashore in his barge, dressed in his best uniform, for a meeting with the Admiral and Governor. As he left, Esi found Marty and told him to join him for a trip ashore with Mr. Evans. They were going shopping to restore the captain's private stores and Mr. Evans was going to buy in fresh supplies for the crew. This was super exciting news, and he knew he would be the envy of all the other boys. So, he raced down to his berth, got into his cleanest clothes, and got back up to where the Purser and Esi were waiting by the larboard entry.

The first came up to them and asked the Purser if he would be so kind as to get the wardroom some fresh supplies and wine. He handed over a list and a purse of money.

"Can I buy myself something when we are over there?" he asked Esi.

"Do you have any money?" Esi replied.

Marty thought for a moment and then said, "Well I get eight pound a year in pay, and there's prize money due, isn't there? After my Dad's share, I'm left about a shilling a week from my pay. I've been at sea three weeks now, so I guess I've got three bob owing me."

"Oh, he's a sharp one," laughed Mr. Evans. "Well, young man, you have to pay for your slops and accoutrements out of that and so I reckon you still owe me money. But cus of yer cheek, I will advance you sixpence on account." He dug in his purse and took out a silver sixpence, which he handed to Marty with the admonishment not to waste it, or worse, lose it. That was more than he expected and more than he had seen in his entire life!

Just then, the gig pulled up at the side and they were asked to hop to it and get aboard. The trip to the dock steps gave Marty time to look around and take in just how formidable Gibraltar was. The huge hill, or mountain in his mind, rose up above them and dominated the whole scene. He could see that there were people stood on the top, and he wondered if they had walked all the way up. The thought alone made his legs ache.

The harbour itself was lined with shops and taverns. There were people dressed in all sorts of strange clothes and a large number of soldiers in their red uniforms and, of course, sailors. He saw that at the top of the stairs was a contingent of the Falcon's Marines under the command of Sergeant Strong.

When they got to the top, Esi said he needed to get some private stores in with a wink to Evans. Evans grinned back at him and took Marty by the arm and said he would take Marty with him. Two Marines were detailed to go with them partly for protection as Evans was carrying a lot of money and also to carry the small purchases that wouldn't be shipped to the Falcon.

They visited a number of merchants where Marty got an introduction to the art of haggling. Evans would tell the merchant what he wanted. The merchant would then show them samples of what he had on offer and how much each item would cost. Evans would look pained and claim that he was being hard done by and offer a much lower amount. The merchant would then cry out that he couldn't possibly sell for that amount as he had a wife and ten children to feed, and they would starve if he sold so cheaply.

He would counter offer a price somewhere in the middle between his first price and Evans'. After a few more rounds of this, they would settle on a price they were both able to live with and seal the deal with a glass of something.

It all seemed to be quite good fun, and both men expected and even looked forward to this dance, but it did take an awfully long time.

When they got to a cattle yard, the process changed a little. The merchant first made extravagant claims about the size and quality of the animals and tried to get Evan's to buy without actually seeing them. That didn't wash. Evans insisted on seeing the beasts himself and when the merchant showed him a pen full of cattle, he poured scorn on their size and quality, all the time casting his eyes over the other pens.

When the merchant dropped his price, Evans appeared to accept it but then went to the other pens and selected the biggest and most well-fed animals in each one and offered up the cash as if they were the animals from the first pen, which were inferior. The merchant howled in outrage and started to refuse, so Evans took Marty by the shoulder and turned them away as if they were leaving. This stopped the merchant in mid-flow, and he ran around them to block their exit, ringing his hands and complaining that the royal navy were robbing him. A new price was offered slightly higher than the amount of cash that Evans had initially offered and after a show of pondering, it was accepted. The chosen beasts were transferred to a separate pen, and the merchant promised to have them delivered to the ship forthwith.

After they had bought all the required stores for the ship, Evans turned his attention to replenishing the captain's and Wardroom's private stores. They visited notably better-quality establishments and cured meats, cheeses, preserves, vegetables, butter, shore bread, and large amounts of wine were procured. Evans loaded the two Marines up with some things he wanted delivered to the captain immediately and sent them back to the boat ahead of them.

Their business concluded, they wandered back in the direction of the port . Marty's stomach gave a loud growl. Evans looked at him with a smile and said,

"Hungry, boy?"

"Yes, sir!" Marty replied, hopefully. After all, it had been a long time since breakfast.

"Ok, let's get some grub then. There's a pub just down here where we can grab something."

The 'something' turned out to be a nice pie of indeterminate content, served with boiled potatoes washed down with lemonade. Pudding was plumb duff and custard. It was far better than the regular food the crew got but not as good as the 'leftovers' he and Esi shared after the captain had eaten. Marty hadn't noticed but in the month he had been under the captain's care, he had showed more growth than in the last six at home. Better and more plentiful food being the main contributor but the exercise he got from weapons practice and skylarking in the rigging was helping develop his body too.

Full and content, the two of them resumed their walk back towards the port. It was still a way off as their shopping foray had taken them almost to the back of the town. As they passed a dark alley, a voice said,

"Stop right there you two!" And two dishevelled looking ruffians stepped out of the shadows with long knives in their hands. Their intent was plain and a quick glance up and down the street showed that no one was around who could help them. Marty looked at Evans, who looked like a startled owl, eyes wide and a look of shock on his face.

So, he put on his best innocent Dorset boy look and stepped toward the nearest man and said,

"'elp me, mister. This bloke has taken me from me Mum!" Confused by the sudden change of role from robber to rescuer, the man lowered his knife, half crouched and put his arm out as if to grab Marty away from Evans. Marty stepped forward as if to go to him but swung his right foot up in as hard a kick as he could manage into his groin. The man howled and doubled up in agony, Marty shoved him as hard as he could into the other man's legs, tangling the two of them together.

"RUN," he yelled at Evans, grabbing his arm, and pulling him towards the port, and run Evans did, as fast as his fat legs could carry him down the sloping street to a busy thoroughfare, which it joined one-hundred yards down.

Safe amongst the regular traffic, the two stopped to get their breath for a moment, then Evans took off at a fast walk to the pier where their boat was waiting. Without a bye, your leave, or thank you, he jumped into the boat and practically dragged Marty in after him, yelling to the crew to get them back to the ship as fast as possible.

Once back on board, Evans left Marty with Esi while he went in to talk to the first officer and then the captain.

"What the 'ell were that all about?" Esi asked. "I've never seen Evans so flustered." Marty told him what had happened with the explanation that Tom Savage had told him if he was threatened by a bigger man to kick him in the bollocks and run like hell. So, that's what he did.

Just then, they heard the captain call for Esi, who went in straight away and almost immediately came back, grabbed Marty by the arm and took him in to the captain's day room. Evans was sat on one of the comfortable chairs with a glass of something dark in his hand looking a mite more comfortable than before.

"Well, young Stockley," said the captain, "I hear you have been at it again! Mr. Evans has enlivened me with a story of daring do and the heroic application of a well-placed kick." He looked like he was trying hard not to smile. "Now, who taught you that form of fighting? It's certainly not in the Navy's manual of combat training."

Marty was, by now, blushing furiously and feeling like he wanted to sink through the deck.

"Umm, it were what Tom tol' me, sor," he admitted his Dorset accent thickening. "He says as I'm so small, to kick the buggers where it hurts and run like 'ell. So, 'at's what I did. Only, I had to put a brake on t'other bugger, too, so I gave 'im a shove so he got tied up in t'other feller's legs."

This was too much for Esi, who started to giggle and then laugh out loud, which set off the captain and even Mr. Evans. All Marty could do was stand there with his ears burning. Noticing his discomfort, the captain stood and came around the desk and put his hand on the boy's shoulder, holding out his other hand for him to shake.

"Thank you, young Stockley,' he said, "for both saving our esteemed purser the embarrassment of being robbed in broad daylight and for lightening a day that has been bereft of any sort of amusement. You can have the rest of the day to yourself."

That was the end of the meeting. The captain dismissed him and Esi, and they went back to the steward's galley. Cox Batrick was waiting for them.

"Does young Stockley have any duties right now?" he asked.

"No, the Cap'n gave him the rest of the day off," replied Esi.

"Come on then, young'un," said the cox and led Marty down to the Purser's Office. Evans met them inside and bade them sit down.

"Young Marty, I have yet to thank you personally for what you did. I have something here that will mean you won't have to resort to such direct methods to protect yourself in the future."

He then reached up to a high shelf and took down a cloth wrapped object that he carefully unwound to reveal a knife in an ornate sheath.

"This is an American Frontiersman's hunting knife," he explained. "It's also a very effective fighting knife."

He pulled the nine-inch blade from its sheath.

"See this pattern on the blade? That shows it's made of Damask steel and is very strong. Then, note the blade. It's sharp on both sides for the first three inches back from the point- that makes it good for stabbing and slashing. John here is the best knife fighter on the ship, and he will show you how to use it."

Marty was a little nonplussed as Evans wasn't known for his generosity but thanked him most warmly once he got over the surprise.

Cox Batrick led him out to an empty spot on the foredeck and told him to put the sheath on his belt.

"You're right-handed, yes?" he asked.

Marty nodded.

"Then put the sheath on your left side with the handle facing forward. That will help you get it out in a hurry until you grow big enough to wear it on the right or at the back."

"Now, take it out and show me how you hold it."

Marty drew the knife and held in like he was going to stab something.

"That's only how you hold it if you're gonna stab someone who's lying down, or you are going to slash backhand," said the cox. "Look, hold it like this." He said holding out his own knife with the blade edge down and his thumb pointing along the back of it towards the point.

"This gives you most options to stab, slash, or block. Now, stand with your feet shoulder width apart with your weight over your toes and knees slightly bent." Marty moved into the classic knife fighter's stance, and the lesson started.

An hour later, and he was sweating and bruised from where the cox had tagged him with his sheathed knife. Marty hadn't got near him with his bare blade. "That's enough for now," said the cox. "We will have an hour every make and mend day. Now, off you go and have some fun."

"Cox?" Marty asked.

"What's damask steel?"

"Aah, as far as I understand, it's steel made in North Africa in Damascus, and it makes the best blades in the world, so what you have there is a rare prize. It will serve you well if you look after it."

Marty just nodded and went off to find Tom Savage to show him. Tom wasn't far away and had, in fact, been watching the lesson rather carefully. He was very complementary about the knife, saying he hadn't ever seen one like that before and it looked like it could do some proper damage. He also cautioned Marty not to use it for his everyday chores, but to keep using his sailor's knife for that as the hunting knife was far too good to be wasted on such mundane things. Marty agreed and then asked if they could practice some knots. His nimble fingers found making the knots relatively easy, but he needed to practice so he could remember all the different types and what they were for. There were three different types of Bowlines, for example. Then, there was the Anchor hitch, Cleat Hitch, Buntline Hitch and many more. So many to learn.

It was around about the end of the lesson that the cry went up that mail had been brought aboard and when he saw Esi next, he found that he had an envelope from Miss Turner. She had written him a two-page letter, which said that his family was well and that his friends were enjoying the summer. His sister, Helen, had asked that she pass on that they all missed him. She was sad to have to tell him that old Ted had passed on peacefully in his sleep and that most of the village turned out to give him a good send-off.

There had also been a summer fete, and Helen was seen walking out with the eldest Cooper boy, and they all expected them to be married in the fall. It was all a bit domestic, and he thought about the letter he had written her telling about his experiences on board the Falcon. He had left out the fight with Smith and glossed over his role in saving the captain's life. He knew that he would have to write her another letter soon and one for her to read out to his family.

Chapter 6: The Mediterranean

They left Gibraltar the next morning on the tide. With the wind from the South West, it was a long set of tacks to work their way up in to the straits. But once out, they could sail large and the Falcon fairly sped along, heading pretty much due East.

From the documents he had copied in fair for the captain, he knew that they were to sail to Toulon to join Admiral Hood. He knew where that was as he had looked it up on one of the maps in the chart room. He also knew that the French revolutionaries were marching on Toulon with a view to capturing it. His inside knowledge made him popular amongst the other youngsters and crew, but he knew there was only so much he could say.

It was three days into the voyage that his nemesis Billy Smith got brave enough to challenge him again. This time, though, he made sure that three of his cohorts were with him. Marty was on his way down to the captain's stores when he found himself surrounded and held by the arms.

"I owes you a thrashin', Stockley, you Captain's pet," he spat and promptly kicked him in the stomach. As the breath whooshed out of him, the two boys holding him pushed him to the deck and all four started kicking him. Marty curled up in a ball to protect his head and took the brunt of the punishment on his back and legs. But one kick caught him in the side of the head and stunned him senseless.

Sometime later, he heard a voice and felt himself being picked up and carried up into the light. As his senses came back to him, he realized it was midshipman Graveny. He was laid on the deck and the surgeon called but before he arrived, the captain, Esi, and the cox all gathered around.

"Who did this boy?" demanded the captain, who looked furious.

Marty knew that if he did say who it was, he would be branded a snitch as well as Captain's pet, and he figured he didn't need that. So, he replied,

"Didn't see them, sir," and then feigned dropping back into a stupor. He heard Graveny saying that he had heard youngers laughing near the captain's storeroom and went to see what they were up to when he found Marty lying on the deck. It was then that the cox noticed that his sheath was empty, and his knife was missing.

Excusing himself, he made his way down to the area of the gundeck where the youngsters had their berth. There, he found a half dozen of them lounging around. He went straight to Smith, hauled him by the shirt out of his hammock, and made him stand. He quickly searched him and then went through his hammock. Nothing. He turned his attention to the next boy and again nothing, the third the same. He moved to the fourth, Toby, a friend of Marty's. A quick body search revealed nothing but when he moved onto the hammock, he felt a hard object in the rolled-up blanket. It was Marty's knife.

"You will come with me," he said and dragged the now terrified boy after him. He didn't see Smith grin viciously in satisfaction.

On deck, he pulled the boy up to the captain and holding out the knife said, "Here's our culprit. Caught him with the knife hidden in his hammock."

Marty by now had been seen by the surgeon and pronounced OK apart from a mild concussion.

When asked what he had to say for himself, Toby could only plead his innocence and say he had no idea how the knife had gotten into his blanket. Marty knew that Toby, who just stood there with tears running down his face, wasn't one of the boys who had beaten him but how could he prove it without an outright accusation?

The captain was determined to stamp out this kind of behaviour on his ship and particularly despised thieves, so he immediately sentenced Toby to kiss the gunner's daughter and take twenty-four stripes with a bosun's starter as punishment. The punishment being particularly severe as it was theft as well as assault. To make it even more educational, he also scheduled the punishment for midday the following day to give the boy time to reflect on his crime.

Marty knew he had just twenty-four hours to prove that Toby was innocent and incriminate Smith and his gang, but how?

The question was, how could he prove that Smith and his cronies were the real guilty parties without snitching? He thought about this and realised he would need the help of someone who could be trusted not to blunder about and spoil it but still have enough standing to be believed. He was excused duties at the surgeon's request, so he did what he always did when he had free time and went to Tom Savage.

Soon, his hands were busy making a splice while his mind was franticly trying to figure out how he could save Toby. It must have shown on his face as Tom stopped him with a touch on his arm and said,

"You know who really took your knife don't you. I don't think young Toby's a thief." It was a statement, not a question, so Marty just looked at him and said nothing.

"You don't want to tell cus you ain't no snitch," Tom added.

"But you don't want Toby to get a thrashing for something he didn't do. Right?" Marty just nodded.

"So, what yer gonna do about it then?"

"Well," he said as the idea he had earlier started to develop in his quick mind

"If I can't tell, then I reckon I've got to get him to give himself up," said Marty.

That evening just after lights out at nine o'clock, Marty was in his hammock along with all the other boys. He waited until it got quiet and then he said "Toby" loud enough for all the boys to hear,

"I ain't goin' to let you get a beatin' on account of Smith an' his mates. It ain't fair."

"Don't snitch Marty!" said Toby. "If you do, nobody will want anything to do with you ever."

Snitching was almost the worst offence a crewman could commit in the eyes of his crewmates as it broke the code of brotherhood that ordinary sailors lived by. It was only exceeded by stealing from your messmates as an offence and could attract severe penalties under the unofficial justice system that operated below decks.

"What you gonna do about it, Captain's pet?" laughed Smith from the darkness.

"Maybe he's really gonna snitch," piped in Farthing, one of the cronies.

"I'm no snitch," said Marty.

Smith laughed and said, "I got you good, you little shit. You can't help him without tellin' and if you do, everyone will call you a snitch for ever."

"You's clever, Smithy," said Short, the dumbest of the four.

"I ain't no slouch," Smith boasted.

"I know how to get even, and I'll make sure you don't have no mates ever no matter what 'appens, an' gerrin Toby carrot head the blame fer nickin' your fancy blade lets everyone know what 'appens to people who is mates with you."

The next morning passed quickly and soon, eight bells were rung to announce noon had arrived. The captain, master, and mids all took a noon sighting and compared notes to fix their position and then all hands were called to witness punishment. Two sailors were brought before the captain for fighting while drunk and were sentenced to loss of Rum and Tobacco rations for a month. A third was brought up on a charge of sleeping while on watch. He was sentenced to twelve lashes as that was a much more severe offence in the eyes of the Navy. Then, it was Toby's turn.

"This boy has been found guilty of stealing a crewmate's knife and assault. Does anyone have anything to say in his defence." Marty stepped forward.

"Toby be my mate," he said, "I know he didn't do it."

"I appreciate the sentiment," said the captain.

"But unless you can name someone else and tell me how he ended up with the knife in his blanket, he will face punishment."

Marty could only stand and say nothing, but then Midshipman Mulhoon stepped forward and said,

"Sir, if I may?"

"Yes, Mr. Mulhoon. What is it?" asked the captain.

"I believe you have the wrong person there, sir," Mulhoon stated.

"Really? And what makes you think that?"

"Well, sir, I was on my rounds last night when I was passing by the youngers' berth just after lights out when I heard them talking. Smith, Farthing, and Short were taunting Marty and Toby as they had trapped them by planting the knife in Toby's blanket. It appears that Smith holds a grudge that he was bested by young Stockley in a one-on-one fight."

"Hmm," said the captain.

"I won't ask why you were there at that time as its not on your normal route, is it? But bring those three boys forward!"

The three were pushed to the front by crewmen stood near to them.

"Are these them?" asked the captain.

"Aye, sir" said the Mid.

"Bring them here," the captain ordered and then spoke directly to the terrified boys. "I will ask you once, and once only, and I want the truth or so help me, it will be beaten from you. Did you attack my cabin boy Marty Stockley, steal his knife, and plant it on Toby Long so he would get a most severe punishment?"

The three quailed under his gaze. He was, after all, second only to God in their world.

Short broke first.

"It weren't me that took the knife, sor," he all but sobbed. "It were Smithy's plan, and he did all that. The rest of us just roughed up Marty is all."

"You snitch!" hissed Smith.

"Aah, the truth emerges," the captain said.

"Number one, do you have any input on the character of these miscreants?"

"Aye, sir. Smith has just got old enough to be rated, but we were reluctant to do so as he is of a bullying nature and has shown a number of flaws in his character. He believes that he deserves to be a topman but although he has the agility, his other faults negate that."

Smith's eyes were like saucers and his mouth wide open in shock on hearing this. He never thought anyone, let alone the first, would have noticed him at all!

The captain nodded and thought for just a moment before saying,

"My verdict, then, in all of this, is that Toby Long is innocent of the charge as laid and that these three miserable wretches are the true perpetrators. The punishment that was handed down on young Long will be meted out to these three in equal measure. Twenty-four lashes each with a bos'n's rattan. On top of that, all three will be put ashore the next time we dock in an English port. I do not want them on my ship any longer than I have to. Until that time, they will work on cleaning this ship from top to bottom and be under the supervision of the master at arms. Bosun, carry out punishment. Make them kiss the gunner's daughter!"

Marty looked across at midshipman Mulhoon, who grinned and winked at him then he looked at the fourth member of the gang, Freddie Salmon, who was doing his best to make himself invisible. The fear of being exposed was enough of a punishment for Freddie, who Marty knew wasn't a bad boy, just easily lead.

The next week passed by quietly and was all the more peaceful as the Smith gang, as they had become known, were separated from the other youngers and made to sleep in the Cable Tier. Word had it that Smith had sworn to get even, but no one took that seriously.

One thing that was noticeable was that Marty's clothes that were loose and baggy on him when he got them from Evans, were fitting much better now. In the eleven weeks since he had left home, he had been fed well, exercised a lot, and had both grown taller and filled out. In fact, he was now growing so fast that Tom Savage said he could hear his bones creak.

He had it in mind to try and tell his mother about that in the current letter he was writing. It was a sea letter where he added a bit everyday like a diary and would be sent the next time the post left the ship. As he didn't know when that would be, he wrote the letter in as small writing as possible. Esi gave him the tip that once he had finished writing one way on both sides, to turn the page through ninety degrees and write across that way to save paper and weight as the post was charged to the receiver by the ounce.

Knife fighting lessons progressed well. He had a natural affinity for the knife and quickly learned some of the nasty tricks that Cox Batrick showed him. Likewise, he learned how to swing a cutlass and use a boarding pike at weapons training although he preferred the tomahawk as it was lighter. He had an idea that a combination of his fighting knife and a tomahawk would suit him well until he grew enough to be able to swing a sword handily. Pistol shooting was beyond him yet as he was still just too small to hold up a Navy Service Pistol with one hand and fire it.

The gunner taught boxing and street fighting to the men and there were regular contests. The boxing had some rules, but the street fighting was vicious, dirty, and deadly and the men joked that as Marty had already shown a tendency to fight dirty, he would be champion as a kick in the balls, a thumb in the eye, or a slap to the ears would all put a bigger man downright handy.

Not least, he attended lessons with Mrs. Crumb every day except Sunday, and his reading and writing were improving. The master had taken over his Mathematics education and was gradually cramming algebra and trigonometry into his young head with the admonishment that he would make a navigator out of him one day.

Soon, they were approaching Toulon and Admiral Hoods fleet. They made their number and recognition signal, and the flag ship responded with 'Captain Report Onboard.' While he was away, they also noticed that there were a large number of Spanish ships in the bay and a large number of French ships in the harbour flying the white flag of Bourbon.

After an hour, the captain returned and called his officers into his cabin. Marty and Esi were handing out drinks when the captain stood.

"Gentlemen," he began.

"I have been briefed by Admiral Hood, and I would like to inform you of our present situation here. The Spanish fleet, you have no doubt observed, is under the command of Admiral Juan de Langara. He is here as our ally along with a large number of Neapolitan and Piedmontese troops, who along with some our own army, numbers some thirteen thousand men to reinforce the French royalists who have handed over the Port of Toulon to us.

The town and port are now about to be put under siege by the republican army commanded by General Carteaux. They have recently successfully quelled the rebellions in Marseille and Avignon and Toulon is now firmly in their sights. They are expected to arrive any day now but no later than the ninth. As long as we hold the harbour, there is little hope they will starve the town out and with the joint fleets here there is also little possibility they can take it by main force. Reports say they have little artillery and not only that, but their Chief of Artillery was also wounded at Marseille, so they lack leadership."

He paused for a drink of wine.

"Our task is to act as a messenger as required and a picket. However, we are blessed with officers who speak not only Spanish but Italian as well."

At this, he nodded to Second Lieutenant Andrew Rampole and Fourth Lieutenant Richard Dicky in turn, who stood a little straighter whilst trying to appear modest. "Gentlemen, you will be required as translators and messengers. You will report to the Flag immediately. Take whatever you need for an extended stay on the flagship. Mr. Gentry, please promote Mr. Smithers to acting Second Lieutenant and Midshipman Fairbrother to acting third. We will have to do without a fourth until I have assessed Mr. Graveny."

This makes Bob Graveny the senior Mid, thought Marty as he watched the looks of surprise turn to ones of satisfaction on the faces of the two young men.

The captain concluded, "I know you will do the Falcon proud every one of you, so off you go. Be about your duties."

That left nothing for Marty to do but start cleaning up the cabin and taking the empty glasses to the pantry.

Chapter 7: Toulon

What the British and their allies didn't know was the French special representatives of the Convention had forced their friend, one Captain Napoleon Bonaparte, on the wounded Chief of Artillery. This despite the fact the two of them had a mutual dislike verging on loathing. The young Captain was out requisitioning enough artillery to carry out a meaningful siege.

For a while, their position looked unassailable, and the Falcon took the opportunity to take on fresh water and supplies. That meant Marty got to go with Mr. Evans on shore for another shopping trip. They didn't need much but any opportunity to take on fresh veg, eggs, and fruit was never missed.

It was while he was waiting outside a shop that he noticed a young man with a rather aggressive stance glaring at him. When he looked at him, the youth spat on the pavement in front of Marty's feet and said, "British cochon." Marty had no idea what that meant but figured it wasn't anything nice and was surprised when a smartly dressed young lady walked up to the youth and started remonstrating with him in rapid French. The youth said something angry in reply and raised his hand as if to strike her. Well, Marty wasn't about to let that go, you just don't hit women, it wasn't done!

So, one second, he was an observer and the next, he was between the two of them in a fighting stance ready to defend the lady's honour! The young man looked down on him with incredulity. Who the hell did this young English fart think he was to challenge he, Phillipe Arnette, a champion of the French Republic! He had just had a savaging from that aristo strumpet and now this pip squeak of an English pig was challenging him? It was too much!

He drew his knife, he was quite proud of his knife, it had been stolen from the Chef of an Aristo pig and been ground to, what he thought was, a fighting profile and looked quite impressive.

Marty heard a gasp from the young lady and looked at the knife in his opponents' hand.

A bloody kitchen knife; is that all he's got? he thought as he slowly slid his knife from its sheath and held it low with his thumb along the top of the blade in a fighting grip. The sight of the nine inches of polished Damascus steel with its wickedly sharp point leading the double edged curved front half of the blade seemed to have mesmerized his opponent. So, he weaved it back and forth a couple of times and watched his eyes follow the blade.

Like a rabbit in front of a stoat, he thought and nearly giggled.

Phillipe, by now, had realized that he wasn't facing what he had thought to be an easy victim who was a lot smaller than him but a trained fighter who had suddenly grown to a frightening size. The thought completely froze him. So, when Marty suddenly advanced and crashed his knife into his blade he found himself disarmed as it was knocked from his hand. Worse that evil looking blade was now under his chin and the point was stinging his throat.

"Do you speak English?" Marty asked. The only response he got was a wide-eyed stare.

"I do," said the young lady.

"Tell this idiot that 'e 'as the manners of a goat and that if I ever see 'im threaten a lady again, I will cut off his ears."

The message was dutifully passed on even though she was obviously having a problem keeping a straight face.

"Does he understand?" He asked, giving his knife a small twist to draw a drop of blood.

She asked, and Phillipe squeaked out a "Oui, madam."

"I sink you can let him go now," she said. "He needs to go home and change his trousers."

Marty stepped back and looked at Phillipe's crotch and sure enough there was a dark patch extending from there down to his knees. He gestured with his knife indicating that his protagonist could leave, without a backward glance, Phillipe picked up his knife and departed post haste.

He turned to face the young lady as he sheathed his blade and asked, "be you alright miss?"

"Mais oui," she said with a curtsey. "How could I be otherwise with such a gallant protector?"

That caused Marty to blush and to cover that up, he asked,

"What was that he called me at the start of all this?"

"'e called you a British pig. He thinks 'imself a brave revolutionary, but they are only brave in a crowd or against people weaker than themselves. 'e must 'av thought you an easy target. May I know the name of my 'ero?"

"Marty Stockley, miss," he replied with a half bow.

She held out her hand and said, "I am the Contessa Evelyn de Marchets."

Not knowing what else to do, he took her hand and shook it, which caused her to giggle again and say, "I see you are not yet schooled in dealing with ladies of breeding. You should take my hand and raise it to your lips while bowing over it and say. 'My pleasure, Madame!' 'Or Your servant, milady'"

"Oh, blimey, miss. I ain't never met no aristocracy before. I be the captain's under steward, that's all," he all but stuttered.

At that point, they were interrupted by Evans emerging from the shop with a huge grin on his face as he had seen the whole thing through the window.

"Now then, young Marty, who be this charming lass you just rescued?"

Marty stammered an introduction, and Evans made a bow over the proffered hand but didn't kiss it.

"Young Marty here makes a habit of rescuing people, but this is his first damsel in distress." He quipped. "He is small in stature but has the heart of a lion."

"I am sure he will grow into a famous warrior," said the Contessa with a smile "Now gentlemen, if you would excuse me, I must be getting 'ome as mamma will worry if I am much longer."

Both man and boy bowed, and Marty watched her leave trying to impress the image of her on his mind. Not too tall with beautiful blond hair, blue eyes, an impish smile, and very ladylike curves, which he was just old enough to notice. She glanced over her shoulder as she walked away with a parting smile, which made him weak at the knees. What he didn't know was that she wasn't more than a year older than he was.

"Well, young Achilles," said Evans. "It's time you earned your keep. I have packages that need to be carried." And the world came crashing back down.

Back on board, the tale of his daring do soon spread, and he was subjected to the good-natured teasing of his shipmates. The other ship's boys all wanted the story in full and made him retell it many times.

The next few weeks were spent out on the edge of the fleet on picket duty sailing back and forth out on the fleet's horizon checking for potential threats and finding none. They did stop and search a number of small cargo vessels but found nothing of interest. Marty kept seeing a beautiful face framed in blond curls every time he laid his head down to sleep and wondered if everything was alright with her and her Mamma.

Then after a month, they returned to port. It was apparent that things had changed. The French had established a battery on the height of Saint-Laurent since mid-September and another on the shore of Brégallion. Rumour was rife that the young artillery commander Bonaparte was gathering a huge amount of cannon to attempt to take the city and the French had unsuccessfully tried to take the forts of l'Eguillette and Balaguier, which would have effectively cut the inner and outer harbours off from each other. A new fort 'Mulgrave' had been built by the British in response to give some added protection.

They continued to spend a month on duty and three days in port for the next couple of months and each time they returned, the talk was about the build-up of artillery batteries by the French.

It was the evening of the sixteenth of December when the shoreward horizon lit up and the rolling thunder of cannon fire heard. All the crew, whether on duty or off, came on deck and all the officers gathered on the quarterdeck. Marty took up his usual position near the steps up to the quarterdeck and watched the light show.

"Sounds like French cannon to me," he heard Lieutenant Gentry say and the master respond,

"Aye, somebody is getting hell alright."

The next morning, a cutter approached them at first light and, after making the recognition signal, came alongside. The Lieutenant in charge boarded immediately and went in to see the captain. He just as quickly returned and boarded his ship with dispatch. The captain appeared on deck and instructed the first to make sail for port and then for all officers to report to his cabin.

Never missing a chance to listen in, Marty made sure he was with Esi as they served coffee.

The captain spoke, "Gentlemen, the French are about to take Toulon. Overnight, they managed to capture all the main forts protecting the harbour and Admiral Hood has decided that the position is now untenable. A general evacuation has been ordered. We have been ordered back to assist.

I want to thank you for your efforts in keeping this ship running as smoothly as it has and let you know that I will be mentioning you in my report. We will be taking back aboard our two wandering interpreters once we join the fleet."

It took most of the rest of the day beating into wind to get back to the harbour and what a site greeted them. The French commanded the heights and kept up a steady bombardment. The allied ships had been forced out of the inner harbour and were retreating out of the outer harbour as they came under steady fire. The captain attended the Admiral immediately on anchoring and returned within the hour with his two wandering officers.

The officers again gathered in the captain's day room.

"Gentlemen, Sir Sidney Smith has been tasked with disposing of the powder hulks and warehouses, and Captain Hare will take the fire ship Vulcan in and burn the French fleet. Our task is to send in boats to evacuate as many of the royalists as we can. Each boat will be armed with a swivel and the crew with cutlasses and pistols. A unit of Marines will be ashore to help with crowd control.

Find out who among the crew have any knowledge of the town and distribute them amongst the boats. I have a list of names who are to be our highest priority. You will each be allocated an equal number to attempt to retrieve, above and beyond them, bring off as many as you can."

At that, they broke up and went to prepare the boats. Marty was given a list of names to split up and copy out into separate lists for three of the boats. It was while he was copying the last one that he saw 'The Comte de Marchets and family'.

Finishing his work, he passed the lists to a midshipman and then knocked on the captain's door with a pot of coffee. Once he had served him, he stood at attention by his desk and waited. The captain noticed immediately that his young servant had something on his mind and said "Well, what is it Martin? Speak up."

"Sir, I heard you say that each boat should take someone ashore who knew the town, and I figured that as I 'ad been ashore with Mr. Evans a number of times like then I should volunteer."

"Oh, did you now?" said the captain.

"Seeking more glory?"

"Oh no, sir!" he protested. "It's just that I saw that we needed to find the Comte de Marchets and his family and as I 'ad met 'em, well one of 'em, I could help, sir!"

The captain smiled at the almost desperate pleading look in his young firebrand's eyes.

"Nothing to do with the fetching Countess is it now?" he teased, sending Marty's ears bright red. He relented.

"Ok, you can go, I know you can look after yourself. My Cox is taking that boat, and I know he will look out for you. Try to come back in one piece and bring her back with you. I need to meet this young lady, I think."

Marty exited the cabin with the bare minimum of decorum and then ran like hell to find the cox. On his way, he grabbed a brace of tomahawks, stuffed one through his belt at his back and the other through the front.

He found Cox Batrick about to climb down into his boat with Evans beside him. Marty blurted that the captain had given him permission to attend. Evans gave a whoop and said, "Love's arrow is buried deep, John! Let's get him ashore to his femme fatale." Marty didn't know what one of them was but as long as he was going ashore, he didn't care.

The harbourside was a mess with crowds of desperate royalists trying to get on board the boats and being held back by Marines. The boat commanders were calling out names from their lists, and those people were let through to board. There was no sign of the family de Marchets.

Marty grabbed the arm of a man who was about to board and said,

"The Count de Marchets, where is he?" The man just looked at him blankly and shrugged, so he went to a young girl about the same age as Evelyn and asked again.

"They are at their 'ouse," she said. "The Count doesn't want to leave his possessions."

"Where is the house?" he asked.

"They live near the Champ de Mars in a big house with golden gates," she replied.

Marty went to Cox Batrick and told him what he knew. After a moment's consideration, he went to Evans, spoke to him then returned with Tom Savage and another crewman.

"Let's go then, boy," he said and led off in the direction Marty had indicated.

The going was slow to start with as they had to practically fight their way out of the docks area, but once clear, the crowds thinned rapidly, and they saw more looters running away with arms full of stolen goods than refugees. They ignored those as they had more important fish to fry.

The Champ de Mars was to the East of the docks and was a neighbourhood of well to do houses, many of which had the doors broken in and the sounds of enthusiastic looting coming from within. It was laid out around a park in the middle with the houses to the outside. They worked their way around until they found a house with large golden gates.

Marty was a bit concerned that they were open as he thought that if the family were at home then they would keep the gates closed and locked. They cautiously made their way up the driveway, keeping a careful watch on the shrubs and trees to either side in case of ambush. When they got to the house, they could see that the door was wide open.

Marty was about to rush in and had drawn his knife and the Tomahawk from the front of his belt when the cox grabbed his arm and put his finger over his lips in a shush. Signalling to Tom and his mate to take position either side and in front of them, he led them forward, weapons in hand. Quietly, they advanced up the steps and paused outside the door listening. When they heard nothing, the cox signalled to Tom and his mate, and the two men ducked through the door and took up position either side of the entry hall with pistols at the ready. The cox led Marty inside, and the four of them made their way down the hall, listening intently.

From a room down the hall and to the left came the sound of someone talking, well, preaching was a better description, in a loud and pompous voice. Marty recognised it almost immediately as the man that he had 'rescued' the countess from. Tom crept forward and glanced around the door, quickly pulling back so he wouldn't be seen. He held up five fingers and then held his hand by his head like the cockade the revolutionaries wore and then four fingers over his heart. Cox whispered in his ear,

"There's five revolutionaries, and all four of the family in there," he said.

"We all need to go in together and fast to take them by surprise. You ready?" Marty nodded. He was scared but angry at the same time.

"Just remember what you learned in training right?"

Marty nodded.

He was ready. Cox held up his left hand and pointed to Tom and then the thumb. He pointed to the other sailor, who Marty now recognised as John Smith the fifth and pointed to the little finger. Marty got the index finger.

The four of them crept up to the door, and Marty and Tom slipped across to the other side. As he passed the open door, he looked into the room and his eyes met those of Evelyn, who just stopped herself from reacting and giving the game away. Instead, she looked Phillipe in the eyes and started berating him just like she did in the town.

That was all the distraction they needed. "At 'em Falcons," yelled the cox, and the four of them poured through the big double doors. They each took on the man in front of them. The cox took the centre left one, who was armed with a musket and bayonet. Tom, the one on the far right, who had a pistol and a sword. Smith the fifth took the one on the far left, leaving Marty the one on the centre right, who was raising a pistol in his direction.

Marty did what he had trained to do, he threw his tomahawk lefthanded as hard as he could straight at the man's face. The Frenchman tried to duck, but they were too close together and it hit him a glancing blow to the side of the head. The pistol went off, but the shot missed Marty by a mile embedding itself in the rear end of a horse in a painting on the far wall. By instinct and muscle memory, his body followed up with an upward thrust of his fighting knife under the ribs of his assailant. Cox Batrick had trained him well. The man gasped and clung to his shoulders and then time slowed. Marty could feel the man's heart beating through his knife and could tell the exact second that it stopped. Even then, the man looked at him with an astonished look, which changed to one of anguish as his life left him and he slid to the floor.

Marty stood there with his bloody knife in his hand staring at the man when a scream pulled him back to the now. He looked up to see that Phillipe had Evelyn by the hair and was using her as a shield with his knife to her throat.

He looked terrified and desperate at the same time. His mouth was open in a silent scream and his eyes were wild and staring at the death and destruction in front of him. This wasn't supposed to be like this! He was supposed to capture the Conte and his family and triumphantly present them to the committee for judgement!

"OY, YOU!" Marty yelled, Phillipe started, then looked straight at him. "COCHON!" he yelled.

"COWARD!" Phillip's eyes widened.

"Think you can take me?" Marty said and placed his knife on a table. He beckoned him.

"Come on, just you and me," he said, stepping closer. Phillipe wasn't biting, he knew he was in danger of his life right now and had seen his brother revolutionary gutted by this terrier like English boy.

Evelyn looked Marty in the eyes, and he gave her the slightest of nods. Marty kept taunting Phillipe and Evelyn kept a steady translation, adding a few choice words of her own, telling Phillipe that even if he killed her, he was a dead man walking.

In the end, it was a barb about him wetting his pants that broke him and, in a rage, he threw her to one side and rushed the apparently unarmed English boy with his knife held dagger style above his head. Marty let him come and at the last minute, dropped to one knee, pulled his second tomahawk from behind his back and in a single motion, swung it upwards into his opponents' groin. The scream that followed was ear splitting and was cut off with a gurgle.

Marty's only concern was for Evelyn. He looked over to see if she was all right and saw that she was in the arms of her father with her face buried in his shoulder. Her father had a look of horror on his face and was looking over Marty's shoulder. Marty looked around to see Cox Batrick wiping the blade of his cutlass on the dead body of Phillipe. When he looked again, he could see that his head had almost been taken off with a mighty slash of the cox's cutlass and was lying in a pool of blood at a weird angle to the body.

He looked at the cox, who just nodded, then looked at Tom, who nodded as well. The fourth member of the team, John Smith the fifth (being the fifth youngest `John Smith on the ship) was wrapping a cloth around a cut to his upper arm. All the revolutionaries were dead.

He turned back to Evelyn and her family and tugged his forelock in respect to the Count and said, "Miss, you and your family need to leave with us right now. You ain't safe here."

The cox stepped forward and said, "The boy's right. We need to leave now. Just grab what you can carry, and we will take you to our boats."

With a face as white as fresh linen, Evelyn turned to her parents and spoke rapidly to them. Pleading for them to listen to good sense. The Count rose and looked at the fallen men, then at Marty and finally at the cox, and in broken English said,

"I zank you for saving my family. My daughter 'as convinced me that we need to leave this, our 'ome, to keep our lives. Please give us un moment to gather some small things we can carry zat will 'elp us survive the trials ahead."

With that the three adults left the room, leaving the youngest, a boy of five or six years old, in Marty's care. Cox sent John Smith the fifth to keep a look out by the front door while they waited. The rest checked out the room for any small tokens they could take as souvenirs. John found a silver hand mirror in a drawer, and it disappeared into a pocket. Marty restrained himself and only took a small porcelain trinket box.

In a matter of minutes, the family returned with three, small, but evidently heavy, bags and some clothes wrapped in bundles slung around their shoulders. They gathered up the child and declared they were ready to depart.

Cox organised the family group in the middle of the four Falcons and they made their way out of the house and down the drive. For a moment, the Count looked as if he was going to go back, but his wife put her hand on his arm, and he turned away. Once out of the gates, they turned towards the docks. The sailors held their service pistols, the Count had a beautifully made pistol in one hand and a bag in the other. His wife and Evelyn carried a small bag each. Marty had his knife and a tomahawk, which he had recovered before he left.

The size of the group and the very visible arms kept most away but they could hear a rising chant approaching from the North, which could only be a large force of revolutionaries approaching the docks. The little boy was having trouble keeping up, so Tom picked him up and carried him as they hurried the family forward. They had just gotten to the harbour entrance when a roar went up behind them and looking back, they could see a mob of people with cockades in their hats waving a variety of weapons running after them.

They were going to be too late, Marty thought as the cox yelled "RUN!"

They all did, the men holding the arms of the women, helping them along, but the mob were almost on them.

"FALCONS DOWN!" Roared the familiar voice of the first Lieutenant. And they threw themselves flat to the ground, pulling the de Marchets' with them. Almost immediately, there was the crash of muskets and the bark of a pair of swivel guns. That was immediately followed by screaming from behind them, as a veritable wall of lead swept the front ranks of the mob down.

"Up and run," yelled the cox, and they dragged the family to their feet, half dragging, half carrying them to the safety of the massed rank of Marines and sailors.

Once behind the cordon, they stopped to gather themselves, and Marty noticed that there were only two bags now. He stepped up behind the Marines and could see the missing bag laying where they had hit the deck. The Marines had reloaded and were preparing for volley fire and the mob were hesitating in the face of it. Marty knew he only had that moment to act in. He pushed his way through the ranks and walked calmly back to where the bag was laying.

The mob was stationary, stunned by the ferocity of the volley that had killed almost all the first three rows of men, and the sheer audacity of the young Englishman. Marty bent, picked the bag up, and slowly walked back to the Marines, who opened a hole for him. As soon as he was behind them, he heard the order,

"By ranks, volley fire! First rank fire!" He didn't need to look to know what effect that would have.

Cox looked at him and said,

"Boy, you have the balls of Odin," and pushed him forward after the rest of them.

They made their way to the boat, which was almost empty. Evans called a greeting and told Cox Batrick that they had taken several loads of refugees to the Falcon, and this was to be their last trip. They got the de Marchets aboard, along with a few other lucky people, then topped up with their Marines who had performed a classic fighting retreat behind the volley fire.

The is positively dangerous, thought Marty as shot splashed into the water around them. The French artillery on the hills was firing constantly down into the harbour, which by now was burning enthusiastically. A huge explosion saw one of the powder warehouses blow up followed by the two powder hulks. They could see the second warehouse was burning but it didn't seem to want to go bang.

They found the Falcon out at the edge of the outer harbour laying to under backed foresails so she could make a quick getaway. Slings were waiting to take the ladies and anyone who couldn't climb the tumblehome up on to the deck. So, unloading was fast and once empty the boats were moved astern for towing.

Once they were all aboard and the ship was safely underway, a message was passed for Marty to attend the captain in his cabin. He was told to enter by the main door not through the pantry. That had never happened before, and it made him very nervous. He was feeling a bit sick anyway as every time he closed his eyes, he could feel the heartbeat of the man he killed in his hand and hear the scream as his tomahawk cut into the other one's groin. But he pulled himself up and shut that away in the corner of his mind where he hid his nightmares.

The sentry stamped to attention as he approached and announced, "Seaman Stockley, saah!" and opened the door for him.

That's a first too, he thought as he entered.

Inside the room, he was greeted with the sight of the de Marchets family plus the Cox, Tom, and John Smith the fifth.

"Aah, young Stockley, come in and sit down," the captain said, indicating a vacant chair.

"Now we are all here, I can formally introduce you to Monsieur the Count de Marchets and his family, who are particular friends of Admiral Hood. Monsieur Le Compt has been personally very active as the liaison with the British Government on behalf of the royalist movement. They have told me of their rescue from the revolutionaries at their home and the trip back to the boats where young Stockley also rescued a very valuable valise in an extraordinarily cool manner."

The Count stood up then. Luckily, he wasn't very tall as he narrowly missed cracking his head on the deck beams, and said,

"Gentlemen, I and my family will be eternally grateful to all of you. Your bravery and dedication to your duty does you and your ship an honour. I would like to reward each of you with a token of our appreciation."

He picked up four purses from the table and handed one to each of them. They clinked in a most satisfactory way and were quite heavy as each held eight Louis d'or gold coins. That equalled around twenty-four pounds! A small fortune for a sailor as it was around three years pay. Drinks were served, and Marty got his first taste of white wine. To his surprise, he liked it. It was cold, as they always kept a few bottles in the bilges to keep cool, and tasted of some sort of fruit, but he didn't know what.

Once the drinks had been finished, the cox and two older sailors were given leave to return to their duties, but Marty was not dismissed, he had to sit tight and see what happened next.

Once they were on their own, the captain turned to him and said,

"This isn't the first time you have had occasion to save Mademoiselle de Marchets' honour, is it?" Marty looked across at Evelyn, who was beaming at him.

"Well, we have met before, sir," he admitted.

The captain laughed.

"Modest as usual. Let me see your knife." Marty drew the knife and passed it hilt first to the captain, thankful that he had cleaned it earlier.

"My goodness, a real fighters' weapon, a gift from Mr. Evans for saving him from being robbed, wasn't it?"

"Aye, sir," he answered.

"You seem to be building quite a record for yourself."

He looked across to the Count.

"He saved my life as well, you know."

The Count raised his eyebrows in surprise and Evelyn gave a small but audible gasp. "He took on two privateer boarders who had me dead to rights. Gave me time to engage them and see them off. Without his intervention, I would be dead."

"Now," he said, handing back the knife, "to matters of import. Your bravery and coolness under fire and the fact that you have saved his daughter not once but twice has caused the Count to take an interest in your future. He considers that a young man of your young years who exhibits such qualities deserves to be given a chance to better himself. So, he has asked that I put you on the path to be an officer."

Marty was stunned. People like him didn't get to be officers! If you worked hard, you might make warrant, but officer? He then realized that the captain hadn't finished.

"So, as of now, I am writing you into the ship's company as Midshipman. I will be sorry to lose your services as my assistant steward, but you will continue to act as assistant to my clerk."

He then reached over to a drawer in his desk and took out a midshipman's dirk. "This was mine when I was a mid," he said. "I would be pleased to see it put to good use again." He handed it to Marty. "You will have to wear it in place of that fighter's blade that you wear now when on duty, but I am sure you will still prefer your old friend to be at your side in battle."

"Now, Mr. Stockley," he continued putting the emphasis on the Mr. "I believe you should move your things into the Cockpit. But first, let me have that purse for safe keeping. It will be kept together with your pay and prize money for the next time you are on shore leave."

Marty stood and remembered to bow to the Count and his wife, grin at Evelyn, and touch his brow in salute to his captain after he handed over the purse. As he left the room, he thought, *Life will never be the same again.* He didn't really know whether to be elated or terrified.

Chapter 8: A New Beginning

His move into the Midshipman's living area, known as the Cockpit, received a mixed reception. He discovered that Mr. Fairbrother had been promoted to Lieutenant. He had moved over to Sir Sydney Smith's ship, the Swallow, as fourth to replace the former incumbent who got himself killed by a piece of falling debris from the exploding powder hulks.

That left Mr. Graveny as senior. Graveny came from a Navy family, his father had been a Captain of some repute before he was killed in action, and his grandfather was a Rear Admiral of the White. He welcomed Marty but obviously didn't approve of someone without Navy connections and such a lack of breeding joining his band of brothers. There was also the fact that it was traditional for new mids to have served at least three years at sea before being made, and Marty had hardly done four months.

The other two mids, Wilson and Muldoon, were also older than him and didn't mind at all as they had met him frequently in their off-duty moments and knew him well. The youngest, Clegg, came from a mercantile family and was a timid soul, quite unsuited to navy life and was acting signal officer. He was only there because he was the youngest son of four and another captain owed his father a favour.

As the most junior, he soon found that it fell to him to do most of the least popular jobs around the Cockpit but thankfully they had a steward. One Matthew Spigot originally from Hull (pronounced 'ull, apparently), who brought them food, served them their meals and cleaned up afterwards.

His uniform was made up of hand-me-downs from the other mids, and just about fit, even if it were a bit baggy and slightly worn in places, but he wore it with pride all the same. He even had a spare shirt.

He wished his family could see him dressed like this as they would never believe it. He wrote extensively about Toulon and his experiences to Miss Turner, and he wrote a separate letter to his family, which he knew his sister, Helen, would be able to read out to them. The mail left soon after as a brig left for England with dispatches from the Admiral and the mail from the whole fleet.

His new duties didn't stop his education but rather accelerated it. He was given a number of books about navigation, theory of ship warfare, mathematics, and so on. He was also 'loaned' an elderly but serviceable Octant. He soon found he was expected to learn how to fix a ship's position by shooting the sun and observing the Lunars (ded (deduced) reckoning) and gross mistakes could result in a visit to the gunner's daughter. He also had to learn the signal book by heart.

If all that wasn't enough, Evelyn took it on herself to teach him etiquette in his spare time! Mind you, he didn't mind that so much as being with her was a pleasure. She also discovered in him a facility for languages and taught him some rudimentary French.

The first lesson he learned in the Cockpit is that midshipmen have a wicked sense of humour. Practical jokes were commonplace, and he found that as the 'new boy,' he was the butt of a lot of them.

He was sent to Mr. Evans for a "Long Weight" to discover it was actually a "Long Wait" when Evans stuck his head out and asked, "Is that long enough?" after he had stood there for half an hour.

He was also told to go and ask the carpenter if he could bring his water hammer to test the well. That earned him a cussing and a rant about stupid mids wasting a professional man's time. He wised up to them fast and managed to avoid the worst.

They had taken on more than three hundred refugees, which made the ship very crowded as that more than doubled the number of people on board. Other ships, like the Princes Royal, were rumoured to be carrying four thousand and in all, almost fifteen thousand people had been evacuated.

Temporary cabins, basically tents, were erected on every spare square yard of deck and facilities were prepared for the comfort of the females. Catering for that number of people was an enormous challenge as they weren't used to ships rations. The captain also worried that if they had to defend the ship against any kind of attack, they would be totally inhibited from operating the guns.

To make things worse, they had a contrary wind that blew from the Southwest that was verging on a storm forcing them to tack to make progress. So, their trip down the Mediterranean towards the Balearics was slow and the sound and smell of three hundred people being dreadfully seasick would be in his memory for ever.

The plan was to offload the bulk of the refugees at Gibraltar where they would transfer to commercial transports for transit to England and the most important to Navy warships returning to England for refit.

Marty found that most of his duties involved running around passing messages and reading signals unless he was tasked with managing a work team. Usually, a clean-up detail after a particularly rough passage.

Because of the overcrowding, he didn't get to work with his gun crews. He did, however, have to learn the gun drill sequences and the tasks of each of the men in a crew. He discovered that he had a real interest in weaponry and became an avid study of all things martial.

Weapons training with this many people on board was necessarily limited, so when the Count offered to give him fencing lessons, he threw himself into learning the subtleties of sword play. Evelyn teased him that he would become a real Chevalier if he kept that up.

The two and a half weeks it took to make their way to Gibraltar went by far too fast and before he knew it, they were dropping anchor in the harbour. At first, he thought that they would be the ones to take the de Marchets to England but sadly it wasn't to be. That task fell to the flag ship, HMS Victory. But none of the refugees would get to leave immediately as there wasn't sufficient accommodation for them on the rock, and the transports hadn't arrived yet. So, they stayed in port, and he had a lively time running resupply missions back and forth, which introduced him to boat handling.

He made the mistake of being overconfident in his abilities. He had watched the other mids take boats out and thought he knew enough, so when asked if he could handle a boat, he said yes.

His first attempt was woeful and attracted an audience that called advice and unhelpful suggestions. As he attempted to take the ship's gig to the dock, he got confused while he was giving orders to the oarsmen and steered the boat out to sea. A hail from the First Lieutenant,

"Mr Stockley if you lose my boat and its crew to the depths of the ocean, I will masthead you for a month!" prompted him to change course.

His crew, who were members of his division, were singularly unhelpful, and he had a strong suspicion that they had been told to only do exactly what he told them to do. *Next time, I won't be so cocky,* he thought.

The cox accompanied him when he commanded the captain's barge and gave him useful tips and instruction. It was a tough way to learn, but he did, and every trip became easier and with three hundred extra mouths to feed, there were a lot of trips.

As he was preparing for one such trip, Robert Graveny took him to one side, passed him a purse and said that the captain had ordered that he visit a tailor and get himself fitted out with new uniforms and shirts.

So, he made his way to Middleton's the Tailors, at the address he had been given, and enquired after his needs. The shop attendant looked him up and down, sniffed, took out a tape measure and proceeded to note down every dimension of his body.

"I assume sir will want us to provide some allowance for growth?" He asked, looking at the cuffs of Marty's shirt, which were up his wrists by over an inch. Marty nodded.

"You will need shoes as well. Pinchbeck buckles, I assume?" Marty nodded again.

"A ship's coat as well please," he said.

"Naturally, sir. The standard purchase for a midshipman is two uniforms, four cotton shirts, four sets of underwear, four pairs of wool stockings, two pairs of shoes, a boat cloak, and a hat. Will you want a belt as well?"

"Yes, please," replied Marty

"And can you add one silk shirt and a pair of silk stockings?"

"Sir expects to get into a fight, does he?" the assistant asked with a smile.

They both knew that silk didn't get into wounds like wool or cotton and cause infections so was the preferred fabric to dress in when going into combat.

"I have something suitable I can adjust to sir's needs that was ordered by another young gentleman who was unable to collect. It will be cheaper than making everything from scratch and quicker. You can pick it all up at the end of the week."

"Umm, 'ow much will all of that be?" Marty asked with some trepidation.

"Eight pounds, five shillings, and four pence," was the response after he added up the list of items.

Marty hadn't looked in the purse yet and looked inside with his heart in his mouth. Inside were six of the gold Louis that the Count had gifted him. That was eighteen pounds!

"I'll pay you half now and the rest when I collect them," he said.

Fishing out two of the coins, he placed them on the counter between him and the shop keeper, whose eyes widened when he saw them.

"I owe you four pound, two shillings, and Eight pence. So, you owe me one pound seventeen, and four; I think." The man stiffened, not sure whether to be offended by this direct approach to money or admire the speed at which this boy had calculated the amount and change.

He went to a Ship's Chandlers and bought a serviceable (almost new) quadrant. Then on to a shop that sold weapons and bought a hanger, which was a short sword, much lighter than a ship's Cutlass with a blade of twenty-four inches and weighing just three and a half pounds. The one he chose was plain but strongly made by Reeves of Birmingham. A real fighting sword with a plain leather scabbard. He also bought himself a lockable sea chest.

After about a week, a convoy of transports arrived, and the ship started to return to normal. He had collected and paid the balance on his new uniforms and now actually looked the part.

Evelyn told him they would be leaving the next day to board the Victory as guests of the Admiral. She handed him a beautifully made wooden box wrapped with a Blue ribbon.

"Zis is for you to remember me by," she told him. "Papa chose zem for me."

Curious, he undid the ribbon and flipped the catch on the front of the box. Inside were two Nock, three barrelled pepper pot pistols with spare flints, powder horn and ball mould. Nock was a London gun maker who was becoming famous for his multi barrelled guns and had started making these around 1790. They were small enough for him to handle and could be carried in a pocket. They wouldn't have a huge range or accuracy but would be lethal at short range. Each gun could be fired three times with the shooter having to manually rotate the next barrel into line between shots.

On closer examination, he realized that the grips had been engraved with the moto "Avec Courage et Honneur" with his name below.

A lump came to his throat, and he leaned forward to grasp Evelyn's hands in his. He made to raise them to his lips when she leaned forward and kissed him on both cheeks.

The next morning, the de Marchets family assembled by the Starboard gangway ready to be loaded into the captain's barge, which Marty had been given the honour of commanding. He wore his best uniform, his dirk, and had scrubbed his face and hands till he shone. The captain was in attendance with the first lieutenant to say farewell and bon voyage to his honoured guest.

The ladies and their son were slung over in a bosuns chair. The boy in his mother's arms. Marty watched with his heart in his mouth as first the countess and then Evelyn came aboard. The count boarded via the entryway holding onto the side ropes. His sword behind him so it wouldn't tangle his legs. Marty stepped forward and offered his arm to steady him. The count looked around, noted that their luggage was already loaded and stowed in the middle of the barge and took the offered seat.

Cox Batrick was in attendance and gave Marty an encouraging nod.

"Let go forward," Marty called and then, "Starboard, side back your oars."

Still held by the aft line, this caused the bow to swing to Starboard. "Let go aft and make way together," he called.

The barge smoothly picked up speed, and he asked the cox to steer for the Victory. As they approached, they were hailed "Boat Ahoy!"

Marty called back, "Le Comte de Marchets and family!"

They were waved to The Starboard entry port, which they smoothly approached, and the bow man hooked on to the chains.

The same method used to load the ladies was employed for getting them aboard, the Count climbed up the battens on the hull over the tumblehome. Last, the luggage was slung aboard.

"Blimey, they must have been shopping." Marty said to the cox as he watched the trunks rise in a cargo net.

Then a voice called down from above, "Midshipman Stockley, please report aboard."

Marty exchanged a look with the cox, who gave him a gentle shove in the direction of the boarding ladder.

"Don't fall in, don't fall in," he kept repeating to himself as he jumped for the first rung and scampered up the side, thankful he had no sword to get in the way.

At the top, he was greeted with the sight of a full honour party still stood at attention and as he raised his hat to the quarterdeck, he asked to no one in particular,

"Permission to come aboard?"

He was answered by an elegantly dressed lieutenant with gold braid hanging from his shoulder.

"Permission granted. I assume you are Midshipman Stockley?"

"Aye, Aye, sir," Marty replied, standing to attention.

"Well then, come with me. The Count asked for you to come aboard and be presented to the Admiral."

He led off aft to the quarterdeck where Marty could see the Count and his family talking to a group of officers. As he approached, he was struck by the presence of one man in particular. He had silver hair and must have been over sixty years old. He had a strong face with a prominent nose and a quite haughty expression. He was in fact approaching seventy years old and had been in the Navy for almost fifty-three years. He was Admiral, Lord Samuel Hood.

"Admiral, sir" said the Flag Lieutenant "Midshipman Stockley."

Marty felt impaled by the piercing blue eyes that stared down at him, but he remembered his manners, bowed, and said, "My Lord." and returned the direct look.

The admiral chuckled and said to the Count,

"I see what you mean m'dear. He has iron in his soul, doesn't he?" Turning back to Marty, he said, "The Count has told me of your service to him; that he is taking an interest in your future and is sponsoring your internship as a midshipman."

Didn't know that! Marty thought, casting a quick glance toward the Count. Sponsoring sounded like he must be paying for it!

"I am returning to England to retire at the end of the year, but I shall still be keeping an eye on things even so and will have some influence. So, do not be afraid to ask if I can aid you in any way."

"Thank you, milord," said Marty, trying very hard not to squeak.

The admiral turned to the Count and said, "You should say your goodbyes to your young friend as he needs to get back to his ship. I will see you once you have finished in my cabin," and then he left.

Evelyn was first to approach him. She hugged him and kissed him on both cheeks,

"Do not forget to write to me," she said with tears in her eyes. "I will write to you every week."

"I will," he said. "Although, you may not get them for a while; the Navy post being what it is."

Her mother was next. She also hugged him and kissed him on both cheeks, saying in French for him to stay safe and to remember to eat enough.

Finally, the Count approached him and took him by the shoulders. To his surprise, he also kissed him on both cheeks and said,

"My dear Martin, I have great 'ope for you in ze future, but don't let your fighting spirit rule your head. You 'ave a great mind and should use it before your sword. Now, go to your duty and make us and your parents proud of you."

Knowing when he had been dismissed, Marty touched his hat brim in salute and giving a fond last look to Evelyn, left the quarterdeck. He turned before going down the entry port, saw them waving from the quarterdeck rail, and gave them one last wave before he dropped out of sight.

Chapter 9: Pirates and Prizes

On returning to the Falcon, he found it a hive of activity as she was preparing to put to sea. Orders had been received, and they were wasting no time in carrying them out. Marty was directed to his division, who were busy stowing last-minute stores that were being delivered aboard by hoys.

The sturdy little vessels were tying up alongside to be unloaded and nets of shore bread, cheeses, barrels of ship's biscuit, baskets of vegetables, lemons, oranges and limes, livestock, in the form of bullocks, goats, hens, and rabbits. There were cases of wine for the officer's mess and one or two for the mids as well. Marty had remembered to get some personal supplies in, and they were delivered along with those of the other mids. Finally, the water hoy arrived to top up their water supplies to full.

Once all that was on board and stowed to the satisfaction of the First Lieutenant, the Falcon was warped over to the gun wharf to be stocked with powder and shot. That was a particularly nervous exercise with all naked flames extinguished, the decks wetted and anything that could cause a spark stowed away.

Then, to a flurry of signals from the Flagship and replies of their own, the Falcon turned her head to the sea and made her way out into the Mediterranean.

The captain wasted no time in making sure his crew were back up to standard in sail tending and gunnery. Exercises were set every afternoon in lowering and raising the top masts, changing sails, tacking, and wearing at unexpected times and as many evolutions as the captain and first could dream up.

Marty found himself climbing the masts to help reef topsails and replace a top gallant spar, then down to the deck to supervise his division at their guns. He was given the aft carronades to manage. He liked these short-barrelled smashers. Despite their thirty-two-pound shot size, they could be managed by just three or four men as they slid back under recoil on a slide, had short barrels, which made loading easy and at anything up to a mile could be devastating. The captain liked to reserve them until they were within a couple of hundred yards as the short barrels made them inaccurate at longer ranges. He had a range of shot he could load; Bar, Canister, Grape, Round, and double headed, depending on what the captain wanted to achieve.

He exercised his gun crews mercilessly, pushing them to be the fastest on the ship. He even had ideas of how to aim the beasts and tried them out with some success against floating targets.

They had been given a cruise by the admiral and had three months of freedom to take as many prizes as they could, but during the shake down period, the captain kept them close to the North African coast as he wanted them at their best when the encountered the French. With a favourable wind, they made good time and were about level with Cartagena near the gulf of Arzew when the lookout spotted wreckage in the water. The captain ordered the sails backed and they hove to a short distance away. Marty and Patrick Mulhoon were ordered out in the Gig and Cutter respectively to check the wreckage out and see if they could find anything to identify it.

By mutual agreement, Marty approached the wreckage from the West and Pat from the East. As they got closer, they could see that it was, in fact, the burned-out keel of a European made ship floating just clear of the surface surrounded by burned out timbers and bits of rigging. Marty had his bow man push the pieces aside as he made his way slowly towards the main piece.

They could see nothing that would identify the ship until the bow man called for them to stop. He had seen something as he pushed a baulk of timber out of their way. Marty ordered two men to help him and between the three of them they pulled a plank from the water. It was passed back to the centre of the boat and once they had it laid across the thwarts, Marty could see that there was writing on it in red with gold edging. Seeing nothing else, they returned to the Falcon.

Once on board, they saw that it was probably the name board of whatever ship the wreckage had been. All they could see were the letters NED with a curved edge before them and a line of gold running vertically after. They were all scratching their heads when one of the crew stepped forward and spoke to the fourth lieutenant, who stepped up to the captain and said something quietly to him. The captain looked at the sailor and beckoned him over.

"You have something to tell us Macintosh?"

"Aye, sir,"

"I believe that be the Onedin, sir," he said with an unmistakable Scottish burr.

"I sailed on her before I was…," he hesitated and then continued, "before I was pressed off her to join the Navy. John Taggart was the skipper, and he usually had his family on board. He had this idea that he could make a fortune by trading wines and olives from Sicily up to Gibraltar and supplies for the British garrison back t'other way."

The captain looked thoughtful for a long moment and said, "I doubt they were attacked by the French."

"Yes, they would have wanted the ship as a prize," chipped in the first.

"That leaves us with the question of who," said the captain

The master coughed and rubbed his hand over his head "Hmm, well I think we could be looking at pirates," he said. "Those musclemen from Africa. They would have no need of the ship. All they be interested in is the cargo and the crew as slaves."

"I think he means mussalmen," said Rampole, the Second Lieutenant, with a smirk.

"I wonder which way they were heading?" mused the first. "If it were mussalmen or barbary pirates, wouldn't they be more interested in goods coming from Gibraltar rather than Sicily?"

"Yes, I don't think they would be interested in wine, as I believe I've heard that they do not drink alcohol," added the captain. "Ask amongst the crew if anyone saw the Onedin leave port while we were there."

"Make it so," the First Lieutenant said to the collected mids, and they scattered to talk to their divisions who were just finishing their lunch. The first mess Marty asked hadn't seen the Onedin at all or even knew of it, so he moved on to talk to the next one. This time, one of his crew named Jackson, a gunner's mate, said.

"Aye, I seen 'er. She were just leavin' as we were arrivin'. I noticed 'er cus she were really low in the water and sailin' like a scow."

Marty thanked him for the information. He didn't know it, but his team always liked that he treated them 'civil like' and thanked them for a job well done. "He were young and from a lowly background like them but he were turnin' into a proper officer," was the general opinion.

Marty reported back to the captain, who had a similar report via Archie from one of the foretopmen.

"So, it looks conclusive that the Onedin left port some twenty-seven days ago. Master, given she appeared to be heavily laden, what would be the furthest she could have got in that time?"

The master went over to the chart room and spread out a chart of the region, got out his dividers, and measured off some distances. He frowned, checked the log, and made some more measurements.

"Well, sir, he could have reached port in Sicily in that time but obviously didn't. So, if we take our position and the prevailing current and work the drift of the wreckage into account, I figure he would have been attacked somewhere between here and here."

He indicated a region between Raf Raf and Cap Serat.

"An if'n I were a pirate I would base myself at Bizerte or Raf Raf which be both nat'ral 'arbours."

The captain ordered them to make all plain sail to the East and also ordered a double watch set. It was early in the year, so the weather could change in an instant and he didn't want them to be surprised.

The next morning after the captain had been in an early conference with the master and first, a string of strange orders were issued. They had to remove the top masts and bring them down on deck. They had to change to their oldest set of well weathered sails. Strips of canvas were painted black and slung along the sides to cover the gun ports, and the Carronades and quarterdeck guns were covered in canvas, which made them look like deck cargo.

He's making us look like a cargo ship, Marty concluded. *This is great fun!*

And that was the general attitude of the whole crew, who threw themselves into making the ship look as un-Navy like as possible. It made a change to be messing things up rather than polishing or scrubbing them.

As they approached the Galite Islands, they reduced the number of visible crew members on deck to that of your average cargo vessel, and they steered a course that kept the coast in sight. They were making no more than four knots. Marty and his gun crews were on standby and sat out of sight around their carronades as did most of the crew.

They saw nothing except a few fishing dhows at first but then one of the lookouts reported that one had taken off to the East at a goodly lick. The captain came on deck dressed like a civilian, which looked really odd. He relieved the first lieutenant, who went below out of sight.

Still, nothing happened as it was approaching sundown, so they reduced sail even further for the night just as a cargo ship would. Still, double lookouts were set and changed every hour.

It was just before dawn when a hushed voice said, "Deck there, I saw something moving out to Starboard."

The first took a night glass and scanned from aft to forward and then slowly back again. "There are a number of boats out there between us and the shore," he reported. "They look to be paralleling us about a mile off."

"How long to dawn?" asked the captain.

"About thirty minutes to false dawn," replied the Master.

"Bring the ship to quarters Number One," the captain ordered. "Quietly," he added.

The men were roused by whispering Bosun's mates. Screens removed and the gun deck cleared for action. The men were kept out of sight, and the guns were prepared as far as they could without running them back to load. The Marines quietly climbed up into the tops with their muskets and swivels.

Marty made sure he had both of his pepper pot pistols on his belt in leather holsters he had stitched up himself. His fighting knife was in a sheath in the small of his back where he now habitually wore it. He also made sure his short sword was hanging free on his left hip and a pair of tomahawks were within easy reach. His team joked that their mid was better armed than the marines.

The thirty minutes to false dawn consequently went by quite quickly and the lookouts soon reported that the 'boats' were armed galleys and that there were seven of them.

Marty peeked over the gunwale, but he couldn't make out details. If he could have, he would see that they were twenty-four oar galleys mounting a single twenty-four-pound brass cannon in the bow and full of well-armed men in robes.

"Stay down and prepare to load with cannister and round shot," came the whispered order.

That was a boat killer of a combined load for a carronade. The round shot were cricket ball sized, made of iron, and weighed about four pounds each. Half a dozen were loaded on top of the cannister, which was a light tin container full of musket balls. The round shot would smash the light timbers of the boats and the canister decimate the crews. They would hold fire until their targets were between one and two hundred yards away.

"Deck there! They are splitting into two groups."

"Damn, they are going to take us from fore and aft. Mr. Stockley get those carronades moved to the stern! Handsomely now!" Ordered the Captain.

Marty got his men moving and grabbed some extra hands from the nearest nine pounders. They got the canvas covers off and moved the two aft most guns to either corner of the stern so that could cover that arc of the ship. Up forward they were doing the same. They were just in time as the four galleys that had split off in their direction were turning and accelerating to attack. Marty could hear the beat of the drums used to set the stroke rate clearly now.

He got his guns loaded and a quick glance forward showed that the canvas camouflage had been cut away and the guns run out. Undeterred, the galleys kept coming and at a range of three quarters a mile he saw the big twenty fours open up on them. Shot splashed down either side, but none hit and the stern chasers below, in what was normally the captain's cabin, barked their reply.

"Close, but no prizes so far," Marty observed and was pleasantly surprised when the chasers got off another round each before the galleys fired again.

This time, they were closer, and one shot shrieked over his head. Now, he could see the men in the galleys waving muskets and swords and screaming war cries.

"Ready lads," he said and instructed his gun captains to go for the two nearest.

"Fire when ready, Mr. Stockley," said the calm voice of the captain.

"Ok, lads! Let them have it!" Marty cried.

The double bark of the guns as they went off and the huge cloud of smoke was most satisfying.

"Stop yer vents, worm, sponge, cartridge, canister, shot, wad, tamp down!" He yelled. When the smoke cleared, he saw that the two target galleys had been hit. The one on the left had taken it right on the bow and the deadly load had passed right up the centre of the craft, causing absolute carnage. The second target had turned at the last moment and taken the hit on the Starboard quarter and had a large hole that the sea was flooding into.

He turned his attention to two more galleys that were getting uncomfortably close and let off their cannons. The stern chasers fired at around the same time and one of the galleys had all the oars on one side sheared off causing it to veer away. But the shot from the twenty-four pounders did their work and there was a horrendous crash from below their feet and the deck bucked as at least one smashed into and through the stern. Marty looked over the rail and could see that both chasers were out of action.

"It's up to us now," he yelled to his men.

"Skin those bastards! Fire!"

Again, they managed to score hits on one of the galleys. The other came on with the other surviving galley, that had rearranged its oars so it could make way. *Damn,* he thought. *They're too close. I can't depress my guns that far!*

"Prepare to repel boarders," he yelled and looked back to the quarterdeck.

"Oh shit! They are boarding over the bows!"

He could see that most of the ship's crew were forward fighting a horde of screaming Arabs who were surging up over the bows. He realized they were practically undefended at the stern, and there was a huge hole the enemy could board through.

Gathering his tomahawks and his team, he led them down to the deck below. They got there just as the first pirates were climbing over the stern.

He dropped his tomahawks, pulled his right pistol, and with a scream that could have been taken for a rather high-pitched war cry, led his men forward. The nine of them formed a line and let off a ragged volley of pistol shot, which cleared the open stern of enemies. But they knew that wouldn't stop them as each of those Galleys must have had forty to fifty men onboard.

Sure enough, before the rest of the men could think about reloading the next wave appeared. Marty turned the next barrel of his pistol into line and let loose a shot almost point blank into the face of a screaming Arab. He turned again, burning his fingers on the hot barrels and shot another that was about to skewer the sailor to his right. That gun was done, so he shoved it back into its holder and dragged out the other.

He was almost too late. His next assailant was towering over him about to slash down with a wicked looking curved sword when he got the pistol up and shot him in the face. His head all seemed to fold in on itself as the forty-five-calibre ball smashed through it from just below his nose and exited through the top of his head. It was too close now for pistol work, so he grabbed his sword and knife and threw himself into the fray.

He seemed to lose himself in a maelstrom of hacking and slashing. He got knocked over and dropped his sword. Groping around he found it but ended up with the sword in his left hand and knife in the right. He lurched to his feet and re-joined the fight as there seemed to be a never-ending supply of attackers and a dwindling number of defenders. Two of his men were down wounded already, another staggered back from the fight with a gaping slash across his chest.

Oh Christ, we aren't going to stop them, he thought.

But then he heard a cry of "At them Falcons!" from behind. Suddenly men led by Richard Dicky the Fourth Lieutenant surged up beside them. After a few more minutes of fighting, the stream of attackers dwindled. Marty, who had just run one through, shoved the doomed man back off of his sword out through the open stern and looked down to see the galleys awash and sinking rapidly. He heard a shout and looked up to see Clegg and Muldoon leaning over the side dropping nine-pound round shot down onto the hulls. He shouted and waved, and they grinned back at him.

All of a sudden, the adrenalin stopped, his legs turned to jelly, and he found himself sitting on the deck in a puddle of blood. One of his men came to him immediately and asked if he was hurt. Marty did a quick inventory of his body and apart from a minor cut or two, he seemed to be intact.

"It's alright. I am fine," he said. "I just need a moment to catch my breath."

Richard took command of the stern to make sure no pirates could sneak back on board, and Marty was relieved to get back on the main deck after making sure that his wounded were taken care of. The crew were unceremoniously dumping the bodies of dead pirates over the side into the sea. He also noticed there were a few ragged looking individuals clustered around the main mast and a few of their own sailors sitting quietly waiting for the surgeon.

Glancing over the side, he saw that all but one of the Galleys were sunk or sinking. The remaining one was damaged, but still swimming tied up alongside.

Mr. Gentry approached, and Marty touched his forelock in salute.

"Are you injured?" He asked, looking Marty over.

"I am fine, sir," Marty replied and indicated the blood splashes adorning his uniform, "most of this isn't mine."

"I am pleased about that. Your prompt action probably saved the ship. So, I am sure that you will be mentioned in the captain's report. In the meantime, there are a number of repairs that need overseeing, including the captain's cabin. So, if you would be so kind as to form a working party, clean up the mess down there and then assist the carpenter in making the repairs."

"Aye Aye, sir," he replied and turned away with a salute to get on with the job. *No rest for the wicked*, he thought with a smile.

Two days later both the Falcon and the Galley were back to being fully seaworthy. The mid's steward had made an admirable attempt to get the blood out of Marty's uniform, but it was a bit of a lost cause and probably needed the attention of a proper laundry.

Oh well, he thought. *It will do for general duty, and for next time we are going into a fight.*

An independent observer who had been watching Marty from the time he had left home to now would note a number of things. In eight months, he had grown three inches in height, had put on over a stone and a half in weight, but more significantly, even though there was still a distinct west country burr, his accent was changing. His siblings would probably tease him that he was going posh, but it was inevitable that this young impressionable boy would pick up the nuances of speech of his peer group. In this case, they were mostly from well to do families.

His muscles had developed, he now had broad shoulders, and his hands had developed calluses both from hard work and weapons practice. He was a scrapper, a fighter who fought to win not to impress, and he had developed the self-assurance of one who had survived some brutal encounters.

Word had it that the captain had some new information as to the fate of the Onedin, and he called all his officers together to tell them what he planned to do next. Marty entered the cabin to the sound of the sentry's announcement of his arrival ringing in his ears. He hadn't gotten used to that yet. He took his place at the back of the room and as there were no seats left, leaned back against the bulkhead. Esi came over and handed him a glass of wine with a wink, he replied with a broad grin.

"Gentlemen, you know that we managed to rescue some of the slaves from the galley that we captured. We found that there were a couple who were British. They have been extensively interviewed by me and Mr. Gentry, and we are now confident we know what happened to the Onedin and its crew. According to the slaves, the Onedin was attacked by the same galleys that attacked us, or at least most of them. Their ship was taken relatively easily as she was heavily laden and unable to out run her pursuers. The cargo was mainly supplies for the army; cartridges and loose powder for muskets, powder and ball for cannon, food stuffs, uniforms, and so on. The entire cargo was offloaded to the galleys. They took the crew, captain and his child captive. His wife was handed over to some of the pirates to amuse themselves. It took her three hours to die, apparently."

There was a general angry muttering at this. Making war on or abusing women went against the grain of most sailors.

"The cargo and crew were taken to the galleys home port of Bizert. Master, please fill us in on that location."

The master stood and came to the front of the room and spread a chart out in front of them. The chart showed that Bizert was located on a natural harbour open to the Northeast. It had an old fort on the Northern tip, but it apparently had no cannon in it. He said the approach was deep enough at five fathoms, but it shallowed rapidly closer in to only two fathoms. There were also some nasty sand bars.

There was a wooden dock where the Galleys tied up backed by storage sheds. Slaves were held further back in the town in a large holding building, which was largely unguarded, because, if a slave escaped, they had nowhere to go and all they did was provide entertainment to the Bedouin who enjoyed a good chase. The rescued slaves had said that there were around a dozen galleys in all and they had the manpower to man them all.

"So," interrupted Mr. gentry. "Given that we destroyed six and captured one, that leaves them with five, around one hundred slaves and probably two hundred fighting men"

"Yes," replied the captain. "That makes a forced landing practically impossible, so we have to come up with a way to free the slaves and destroy the cargo from the Onedin that doesn't involve a land battle we cannot win."

Lieutenant Smethers raised a hand and when the captain nodded to him, said, "Sir, is this not a classic problem that can be solved by misdirection? I mean, can we not make the enemy believe that we are attacking them from one place while a small force takes on the main task of freeing the slaves and burning the store houses?"

"Go on," said the captain intrigued.

"Well, if we stage a landing on the beach here to the North of the town," he pointed to the beach on the map, "we could draw their forces out and if we could defend the beachhead for long enough, a small force could enter the harbour using the captured galley and carry out the rescue and demolition."

At this point, he looked to Lieutenant La Pierre of the marines, who was looking thoughtfully at the map.

"Mr. La Pierre?" prompted the captain.

"What we could do," he said thoughtfully "...is bring a contingent of Marines and armed sailors on to the beach here just North of the town. We arm them with muskets, bring as many swivel guns as we can, and establish a beachhead. If the Falcon could be stationed just offshore, anchored with springs, the landing could be supported by her artillery. That should be defensible for as long as it takes the raiding party, also made up of marines and sailors, to rescue the slaves and set fire to the storage sheds say an hour maximum."

Lieutenant Smethers chipped in again.

"I see one problem, sir. We will need all the boats to land the party on the beach, but we will also need them to take off the rescued slaves."

"Hmm, I see what you mean," said the captain.

Marty had a sudden inspiration, "Excuse me sir, but why can't we use the galleys that are at the dock to take off the slaves? They know how to row them after all."

"Ha, expect a mid to point out the obvious fact that we all missed!" laughed the Captain. "Gentlemen, we have a plan. Now, let's work out the detail."

It took them a further two hours to work out the details and to allocate all the preparative tasks. Marty was given the galley. They had decided that it would be better served with a pair of carronades rather than the big, hard to manage twenty-four pounders.

His first task was to get the huge beast out and up on to the Falcon's deck. The gunner had inspected it and declared that it was in good condition, and it could make a good price at the prize court. Weighing in at around two and a half tons it presented quite a challenge to hoist on board. With the help of the experienced bosun's mates he had in his work party, a suitable arrangement of blocks and tackles was assembled that enabled the barrel to be hoisted slowly aboard, followed by the carriage. Both parts were sent down into the hold for storage. The stone balls were thrown overboard, the powder kept as it was originally from an English ship and was good quality.

The carpenter created two platforms, one on either side of the bow to mount the carronades and to give sufficient room for the gun crews to work. This had the added benefit that the two carronades weighed roughly the same as the twenty-four pounder, so the trim of the craft was maintained. The carronades could be traversed by about twenty degrees either way.

They stored cannister and grape shot just aft of the guns where the stone balls for the twenty-four had lain. Cartridges were stowed in barrels beside the ammunition for want of anywhere else to put it. Marty carefully stowed a pack containing signal rockets, slow match and a spare flint and tinder under the foremost bench.

A crew of oarsmen were assembled, supplemented by some of the rescued slaves who volunteered to go along. The rest of the raiding party was made up of a squad of eight Marines commanded by Sergeant Strong and twenty sailors. Overall command was given to the Third Lieutenant, Mr. Smethers. Marty was to command the guns, secure their own galley, and to capture and hold two more whilst the raiding party did its work. Any other galleys in port were to be burnt.

Once all preparations were complete, the Falcon set sail towards Bizert at a leisurely pace. They wanted to make landfall at the beach sometime shortly after dawn. The Galley would be dispatched an hour before first light to make its way to the East of the port so it could appear to be approaching from the opposite direction to the fighting when it started.

The ship was a hive of activity around an hour and a half before dawn. Men were checking their weapons and getting a last edge put on them by the armorer at the great sharpening wheel that had been brought up from below.

The Marines were being inspected by Lieutenant La Pierre and being given their last instructions. Swivel guns were prepared for loading into the boats.

Marty made sure he had both pistols, his fighting knife, and his sword. He had meticulously cleaned and reloaded his pistols and fitted new flints. He had not primed them as standing orders were that no guns were to be primed until the landing party was at its destination. That was to prevent accidental discharges which were dangerous to the crew and gave the game away. He checked his gun crews and made sure they were appropriately armed and that the gun captains had extra lengths of linstock safely stowed away in oiled canvas bags as a backup.

He had a last word with the gun crews that were staying behind and would be under the temporary command of Simon Clegg. He was tempted to tell them to look after him, but he knew he would hate it if someone said that for him, so he just admonished them to work with Simon like they did for him.

Then he heard the command to heave to. The fore sails were backed, the ship came to a halt, and Lt. Smethers give the order for the galley to be brought alongside. They were quickly aboard, and the oarsmen soon had her moving to the slow beat of the drum. Once they were clear, the beat increased, and the nimble craft fairly leapt ahead. Marty made sure the barrel containing their cartridges was covered in oiled canvas to keep it dry one more time and then settled down for the trip. The course was set by compass bearing and a lookout was kept toward the shore for any lights. There was a quarter moon, but, by this time, it was well down on the horizon, so didn't help much at all.

As the first sliver of dawn hit the Eastern horizon, they slowed their stroke rate and steered a smooth arc to reverse their course. It had to be said they weren't really sure where they were, they just hoped they were far enough to the East of the port that they arrived back on time. He looked back along the galley and smiled as he saw that the Fourth Lieutenant had an Arab robe over his uniform to disguise their identity for as long as possible. Twenty minutes later, they spotted the bay ahead of them.

"Damn, we are early," he said to no one in particular. Suddenly, a lookout, similarly clad in an Arab robe, announced that he could see the topsails of the Falcon and they all heard the thunder of the battery of nine pounders being fired by broadside. Part one of the plan was under way. Now, he knew, the Falcon was lying to and the boats were taking the beach party ashore. The broadside would have been aimed at the houses on the Western edge of town and was to get the attention of the defenders as much as to cause damage.

Not so early after all, he thought as the drum picked up the stroke and they made their way towards the entrance. As they rounded the headland and caught their first sight of the harbour, they could see that the Bedouin were streaming out of the town towards the beach and the landing party. The plan looked like it was working.

One hundred and fifty yards from the shore, the order came to stand by. Marty and his gunners took up position at the carronades and loaded them with grape over canister. The guns were primed, and Marty told his men to prime their pistols.

Seventy-five yards from the shore they could see that there were three galleys tied up end on to the low dock and to his relief he saw that his guns would be higher than the walkway, and when the shore party left, he would gain another few inches of elevation to work with as their weight came off the boat. Fifty yards in and they slowed, nobody was taking any notice of them. Twenty-five yards, fifteen, ten they docked with a gentle bump and the shore party leapt up and onto the dock, weapons at the ready. One of the released slaves ran beside the lieutenant to guide them to the slave's quarters.

Once they were clear, Marty gave the order to secure two of the other galleys and to prepare the third for burning. He jumped up on the dock to get a better view, as there was a lot of noise coming from the area of the beach. Musket shots, the crash of artillery, the bark of swivels, and the screams of men. He could also see smoke and noted it was drifting towards him as the breeze was from the West. He turned his attention back to the direction the shore party had left in.

Time seemed to have slowed. All was still, when suddenly there was the sound of a shot and then another. A Bedouin on horseback appeared at the end of the harbour. He stood in his stirrups and took a long hard look at Marty, just as a half dozen slaves came running out from between two of the storage sheds. The Bedouin took one look at them, turned his horse and galloped back in the direction of the fighting. About three minutes after that, there was a regular crackle of fire from the direction of the prison.

Christ on a crutch, he thought (an expression he had heard from one of the older mids).

"The game's up," he shouted to his crew as he ran back to their Galley.

"Get those guns around so they cover the approach to the dock on the Western end," he yelled. Turning back to his gunners, he told them, "wait until you see me signal before you fire your first rounds. Jack, you fire first, twenty seconds later, Toby, you fire next. That way, we hit the second wave as they are just coming out in to the harbour. Keep up a staggered fire until I tell you to stop." With that, he ran along the dock to the end galley.

Jack looked at Toby and grinned, "He be a right firebrand, ain't he?" He joked. "A proper Dorset boy, they'm all scrappers or 'orse traders." Both men laughed at that.

They had moored their Galley with the two they were commandeering to their left and the one they would burn to the right. This enabled their guns to cover the approach to the dock from the West while still allowing the released slave and shore party to approach from straight ahead. Marty crouched down and watched the far end of the dock. He shrugged and jumped down in to the galley with his men.

"All loaded and primed?" he asked. Most nodded and a couple sheepishly took out their powder flasks and primed their guns. Marty took out his pistols and checked them. A glance over his shoulder showed him that the first slaves were reaching the galleys and a shout alerted him that trouble was approaching from the West end. A half dozen horsemen had appeared from between two buildings and had stopped as if assessing the situation.

He waited. There was now a steady stream of people running across the docks to the galleys. One of the horsemen raised his long musket and fired. There was a scream as one of the slaves fell. "Hold!" Marty shouted. More men joined the group and then after a quick look over their shoulders, the horsemen started forward. He waited until he could see more men emerging onto the dock and yelled.

"Jack! Fire!" The carronade barked, and a cloud of smoke and flame erupted from its barrel. The effect of the grape and cannister on the leading group was instantaneous and devastating. Men and horses screamed as they were ripped apart. The following men kept coming screaming their war cries and waving their weapons. The second carronade spoke, and another wave of men were ripped to shreds. They were reloading too slow! He raced back to the galley.

"You men," he shouted to the oarsmen, "who has a musket?"

About half indicated they had.

"Get your arses up to the end Galley and set up a firing position along her beam."

He jumped in behind them and called, "Prepare to fire, aim low, and FIRE." The dozen muskets went off in a fairly even volley.

"Reload" he yelled, and the men went to their business with a will.

About twenty seconds later, the first carronade spoke again, and the cycle repeated itself. But he could see it still wasn't going fast enough even with the musket volley filling in.

The Bedouin were slowly making ground even though their losses were high. He glanced over his shoulder and saw the eight Marines commanded by Sergeant Strong setting up in two ranks midway between the dock and the storage sheds. The front rank knelt and fired a volley. The second rank stepped through to the front and knelt while the now rearmost rank reloaded. The front rank carefully presented and fired.

He realized it was time for his men to fire again and looked around to see a small group of Bedouin racing towards them. He gave the order, but the men were flustered, and the volley was ragged, some shots must have gone high as three were still coming.

"Reload," he yelled as he jumped up on to the dock with a pistol in each hand. "SHIT," he shouted as he fired first his right and then his left guns. One Bedouin fell but the other two kept coming. He dropped his guns and drew his sword and knife and was just bracing himself to fight when there were half dozen bangs from just behind him and the two Bedouin fell with red roses of blood appearing on their chests.

"Jesus Christ!" he yelled as he instinctively ducked.

A broad Irish accent answered him, "No sir, but I tink de Virgin Mary be lookin' out fer your wee soul."

He looked up into a grinning sailor's face, that only a mother could love, and then around at the other sailors who had leapt to his defence holding smoking pistols.

He grinned at them and then turned his attention back to his sailors.

"Ready boys, and this time, point them at the bloody enemy! FIRE."

What seemed like an age later and with his mouth dry from shouting the volleys and tasting of sulphur, he heard the lieutenant call recall. The store houses were well ablaze and the crackle of exploding cartridges could be clearly heard.

Marty led his men back to his galley, not forgetting to set fire to the pile of combustibles in the middle of the spare galley. He noticed that three of the men were being helped by their shipmates and one of them was being practically carried. Suddenly, one of the storehouses exploded, sending debris high into the air as kegs of powder were set off.

Back on the galley, he found his gun crews and laughed at their blackened faces.

"Mr. Stockley," called the Lieutenant.

"Would you be so kind as to send up a green rocket?" That was the signal to the Falcon that they could withdraw. Marty dug around in the pack they had brought on board and found the rocket. Jack, one of his gun captains, offered him a burning linstock. Holding the rocket between two fingers, he lit the fuse. WOOSH! It launched upwards and flew up and over the retreating Galleys.

A half hour row saw the three galleys approaching the Falcon. The view of the beach showed the ferocity of the fighting. There were dozens of dead men and horses. The ship's boats were alongside, and men were climbing up boarding nets that had been slung over the side. Slings were lifting the most severely wounded aboard.

They waited their turn then drew alongside and unloaded their wounded then their human cargo, and, finally, the crew. The First Lieutenant ordered the galleys to be set adrift and burned.

Marty was asked to provide a written report of his part of the action and what he observed. He made sure he wrote it in third person, kept it to the facts, and mentioned the names of his gun captains and any other men that carried themselves with distinction. He heard from the other mids that they had lost men in the action on the beach and would have lost even more if about a third of their attackers hadn't returned to the town to try and stop the slaves from escaping.

He was told by Mr. Smethers that they had gotten almost all of the slaves out of the prison when about twenty Bedouin had appeared and started shooting, killing several slaves and wounding a couple of his sailors. That forced them into fighting a rear-guard action covering the retreat of the slaves. When they heard the carronades open up from the direction of the dock, he had sent the Marines forward to make sure the slaves could reach the galleys.

That evening, the captain had all the officers who manned the beach and rescue parties to dinner in his great cabin. He worked his way around the table complementing each man on his performance until he got to Marty.

"Mr. Stockley," he said.

"I am curious. What gave you the idea of a rolling barrage with two carronades and a dozen muskets?"

"Sir, I saw how the Marines practiced volley fire in ranks," he inclined his head to Lieutenant La Pierre, "and it just seemed that each carronade is like a rank of muskets the way it throws canister and grape. I just figured if I could get them to fire about twenty seconds apart, it would have the same effect. Problem was the gap before the first one fired again was too big, so I got all the men with muskets to line up and fill in with a third volley. But even that were too slow and we nearly cum unstuck."

"Then when the good Sergeant Strong arrived with his Marines, they filled in the gap." The captain finished for him. "Gentlemen, it seems we can all learn from observing how others in the service carry out warfare. I give you a toast. 'To our young men, may they ever surprise us with their ingenuity.'"

"Our young men," roared the rest and tipped their glasses back to heel taps.

"One more toast," said the captain.

"According to the official dates in our muster book, it is Mr. Stockley's birthday today. He has reached the admirable age of thirteen years! To Martin Stockley, a Happy Birthday!"

At this, all the men rose to their feet and raised a glass to Marty, "Happy Birthday, Martin," they cried and gave him three cheers and a tiger.

The meal continued with stories of what had occurred that day, some funny and some poignant, and, at the end, Marty, being the youngest, was asked to give the Royal toast. Clegg, who was a couple of months younger, wasn't at the dinner due to having been knocked over and injured by one of his gun crew during the action because he was standing in the wrong place. To say he slept well that night would be an understatement. He had, after all, drunk more alcohol in that one dinner than he had in his entire life.

The next morning was nowhere near so much fun as he discovered the penalty for drinking too much wine and port. His mouth tasted like he had gargled gun powder and his head was pounding. He felt sick and loud noises hurt. Lucky for him, he had the second watch on signal duty so could spend some time recovering. The wretched look on his face caused the Second Lieutenant, who had the watch to grin openly.

"Mr. Stockley seems to be feeling the after effects of his debauchery of last night," he joked to the others on the quarterdeck. "Never mind, younker," he laughed, slapping him on the back. "You'll get over it."

Marty almost headed for the lee side to cast his accounts to Neptune, but a few deep breaths steadied him. He looked around the ship.

Darn! Are we fated to always have a cargo of refugees? he thought as he looked at the fifty or so slaves sitting or standing around on the deck. They had rescued eighty-six, but some were too sick to come on deck. *These were the lucky ones,* he thought. There were at least a dozen that the pirates had killed while trying to stop the escape.

The skipper of the Onedin and his young daughter were there. He had lost everything except his life and that of his daughter and the loss showed in his face and demeanour. He looked up at Marty and nodded before turning away, head down with a shuffling step.

As they were closer to Sicily than anywhere else, the captain decided to call in there to offload the slaves into the care of the governor. However, once they got there, they found it wasn't so easy.

It seemed that no one wanted to take responsibility for such a large number, and would only take those that could prove they had originally come from Sicily. In the end they could only leave around forty after spending several days finding family members who could vouch for them.

A quick survey revealed that another twenty-eight were from Italy and the rest were from Britain, France, Sweden, and Holland. Passage was arranged for the Europeans on cargo ships heading to their home countries where they could and England where they couldn't, paid for by the captain out of his personal funds. They arranged to send their mail on one of the freighters, but none was waiting for them; much to everyone's disappointment.

That done they headed over the straits to Cannitello, where they left the Italians giving the burghers of the town no choice but to take them.

Resuming their cruise they headed North up towards the French coast in search of prizes. The plan was to stay to the East of Sardinia and Corsica, stopping every ship they saw, then circle around to Monaco, and finally make their way down the coast towards Spain. They would stop off at Mahon to resupply as Spain was still an ally.

It wasn't long before they started encountering cargo ships and the call to clear for action was ringing around the ship. The first couple turned out to be out of Naples, so they were left unmolested, but as they got up closer to Corsica, they found their first French victim. A single shot was enough to see the colours come tumbling down and for them to heave to. A boarding party was sent over under the command of Midshipman Wilson, and Archie waved and grinned to Marty as he was rowed across. It was a single-masted vessel with lateen style sails. It was well used and scruffy, but the rigging looked sound and taut. After about thirty minutes, Archie returned and reported that she was the Esme and they were carrying leather and cordage, there was a crew of five including the skipper, all of whom were Corsicans, they had been heading to Naples.

The captain decided this one was a keeper, so he sent Archie back to take charge of it with a four-man prize crew. *Lucky git* thought Marty, freedom from orders, a crew of his own, damn, that was what he wanted.

The next was a tougher nut. They spotted her just North of Bastia heading Northwest. The weather wasn't brilliant, the visibility was low, and the wind was veering from North to Northeast and squally. She was quickly identified as a Xebec, was fast and able to sail closer to the wind than them. She had Square sails on her main mast, which was in fact the fore, and lateen sails on the mid and mizzen masts. Initially they weren't sure whether she was a French warship or a merchantman. But as the captain said, they would worry about that when and if they caught her.

It was a bit of luck in the end that brought her in range. She ran into a squall, which shredded her top and forward lateen sails and before they could replace the canvas, the Falcon was in range for a shot. The gunner put one from the Starboard fore-chaser right under her bows but that didn't convince her captain to surrender. They just kept right on changing the canvas.

"Mr. Mulhoon." Called the first. "Once we are within a cable, please serve her rigging with a load of bar from one of your carronades, please."

Pat had a grin like a kid who had dug into the plumb duff at Christmas and found the silver sixpence. He took great pains to lay the gun just right and then with the usual boom/chuff, he let it go. The effect was impressive. The bar came out of the carronade like shot from a short-barrelled blunderbuss. The Xebec's rigging around the mizzen was shredded with blocks falling to the deck and huge chunks taken out of the mast. The fact that it hit just above the captain's head had a profound effect on him. He threw himself to the deck with his hands over his head as it screeched above him and when he had finished dodging falling rigging, he ran to their colours himself and hauled them down.

This time, it was the Fourth Lieutenant Richard Dicky who had the honour of leading the boarding party of six Marines and eight sailors. With the Falcon hove to beside them, it wasn't expected that the French crew would give any trouble, but it was better to be safe than sorry. After an hour or so, he returned and reported to the captain that the ship was the Bouvet out of Marseille, and she was carrying a cargo of cloth, spices, Italian glass and Italian furniture.

Not military but worth something, Marty thought.

"Another keeper." The captain agreed with him, and Richard headed back over with orders to make her seaworthy and take command.

Their little convoy continued to head towards Marseille when the Mediterranean threw one of its seasonal tantrums. The storm swept in from the Northeast with a vengeance and within an hour, they lost touch with their prizes as visibility dropped to almost zero with driving rain and huge waves. They were reduced to triple reefed topsails alone and ended up having to run before the storm to survive. During that time, they lost one man overboard with no hope of recovering him. During Marty's watch, he had to tie himself on with a lifeline.

After three days, the wind dropped, and the waves started to settle down to a long swell. After another day, the clouds cleared and allowed for a noon sighting. At first, Marty thought he had gotten it terribly wrong but a glance around saw looks of consternation on all the mids' faces, so he quickly double checked his calculations. Yes, it was forty-one and a half degrees, he submitted it to the master. That put them somewhere off of the coast of Spain between Girona and the Southern tip of Corsica. They would get an idea where along that line they were if they could get a lunar sight that night.

The captain's orders were that if they got separated to rendezvous at Mahon, so they set a course South by Southeast with the wind on their quarter and proceeded at a stately five knots.

When they arrived at the entrance to Mahon, Marty saw from the map that they were slowly approaching what was an inlet with a large fortification on the Southern side of the entrance named as the Castle St Phillipe. They had to move up the inlet to the town of Mahon and according to the master, anchor either at Punta de Fonduco or North of the town at what had been the British naval base. The British had owned the island and this well sheltered natural port since around 1708, but it had been given back to Spain in 1783 as part of the treaty of Paris. It was strategically important to the British due to its position, and the captain had told them that if the Spanish ever sided with the French then they would have to take it back again.

A pilot came aboard soon after they entered the mouth of the inlet and steered them up to Fonduco where they dropped anchor in what looked like a harbour within the harbour. They immediately set to work repairing the damage the ship had suffered during the storm.

Marty was a little disappointed that he didn't get to accompany Evans on his shopping trip into Mahon but as Lieutenant Rumpole spoke Spanish, it fell to him. He wasn't idle though; he was put in charge of the crew to repaint the ship's rails and gunwale and make good the ravages of the Mediterranean winter. He also practiced his knife fighting with the cox, had his lessons to do with Mrs. Crumb and the Master and helped the captain's clerk to make fair copies of the reports to the Admiralty.

He finished his latest set of sea letters and put them in the sack ready to be sent ashore for the next ship bound to England or Gibraltar.

The Captain had decided they would wait for the prizes to join them. As Mahon was friendly to the English and not the French, they would leave the prizes there with skeleton crews and make another patrol up the coast towards Toulon to see if they could discomfort the French in any way. They would return to Mahon after a month or so to refresh their stores and pick up the prizes before returning to Gibraltar.

Evans and Rumpole returned and there was a cry of "MAIL" from the gig as they approached, which caused a great deal of excitement. The bags were brought aboard and taken down to the captain's cabin where his clerk and the first would sort through it. He would have volunteered to help them, but the first of Evans purchases arrived in a barge and he was tasked with the unloading.

That evening, he had some time to himself and he sat himself down between his larboard carronades to read his letters. There were two from Miss Turner and one from his sister, Jane. There was also one from the Count and another with dainty writing from Evelyn. He decided to save Evelyn's to last and opened the letter from his sister. Her writing was never good, and it took him a couple of seconds to adjust to her spidery scrawl. She said,

Dearest Marty,

I hope you is well and bain't got yerself into any more mischief. Mother is missing you and sends her love and so do yer sister Jane. Yer brothers are all working down the pit and wishin they were as lucky as you. Miss Turner gave us the letter you sent us and I read it out to all the others. They are all wondered where Gibraltar be so Miss Turner brought over the atlas book and showed us. Did you really kick that bloke in the balls? We laughed all evening at the thought of that. Mum says to stay out of trouble and not get in to fights. Grandpa Absalom has come to live with us as Grandma Rose died of the flux in November and what with Dad being the oldest son it falls on us to look after him. Tom's wife Sarah is pregnant with their second, and we hopes that she do have a better time of it than the last one. But that were a wedding night baby and were born only seven months after they was wed so I hopes this one do go for the full nine months. (*Hmph the last one went nine month as she was all but showing a bump during the service,* Marty thought). I be lucky too as I is goin into service with the Banks family up at Corfe Castle. It means I will have to live in at that big old house of theres. (She never could tell there from their, he laughed to himself). So next time you writes Helen will have to read it out.

Miss Turner did give Pop the money you sent home and he bought me a new dress to go to the Banks with.

Sendin' all us love and a kiss from Ma yer luvin sister Jane.

That confused him as he wasn't aware of any money being sent home but he put the thought aside to dwell on the rest of the letter. *Well, Grandma Rose passed on,* he thought. *It's a surprise she lasted this long what with having had twenty-six babies.* Grandma Rose had indeed had all those babies including two sets of twins, but only twelve of them grew to adulthood. Life was tough, and the infant death rate was around fifty percent. The fact that Grandma Rose lived as long as she did to near sixty-five years old was unusual.

He opened the one with the earliest date from Miss Turner next. She told him the news from the village and that she had new children at the school. She also said she had received a letter from her brother, who had told her about the incident with the French privateers. She thanked him for his intervention but abjured him to think before he threw himself into harm's way. Her brother had also sent her a note on his bank for half of Marty's pay for her to give to his father. *Ah, that clears that mystery up, then,* he told himself.

The second letter was much the same as the first, but she also told him that she had the good fortune to be able to recommend his sister, Jane, to Mr. Banks, the Squire of Corfe Castle, as a maid of all works, which explained how Jane had got the position. She also read the letter he sent his family and although the thought of Marty defending the purser from ruffians didn't surprise her, the method did. He got the feeling she didn't approve.

He opened the letter from the Count and saw that it had been written from the Victory. The Count wished him well and again thanked him for saving his daughter. He informed Marty that they would be living in England by the time he got back, and that they would make sure they told him where so he could visit. He also told him that he had set up funds of twenty pounds a year for him until he reached the age of twenty-one or he was promoted to lieutenant, whichever happened first. The funds could be drawn on by him from any branch of Coutts bank. The first year's money had been given to the Captain for administrating. He encouraged Marty to keep at his education and to learn his trade well, as he believed he had the potential to go far.

"Well, damn me!" Marty said out loud, prompting inquisitive looks from those within hearing. Twenty pounds a year plus the eight of his pay plus his share in the prizes! By god, he was almost wealthy!

The last letter was from Evelyn. Her script was elegant and small, and it was sealed with pink wax. She called him "Mon cher, Martin." She told him about the Victory, that they had a lot more room and proper beds and the food was wonderful as there was a proper chef on board.

No doubt thought Marty. *That bloody ship was 10 times the size of the Falcon.* He was feeling put out and defensive towards his ship and almost stopped reading the letter at that point. But it drew him back and he carried on. It got worse! She went on at length about how gallant the ship's officers were and that there were many midshipmen of all ages. But then she wrote "but then, mon Martin, it would be perfect if you were here, and I miss you a lot." She told him that she had told the tale of their rescue to her new shipmates and how brave he had been.

Oh Lord, he thought, *I hope I never meet any of them. It will be too embarrassing.*

She closed her letter with a fervent wish that he visit them as soon as his ship got back to England as she longed to see him again. He finished his reading and folded the letters back up. He wondered what she would make of the last letter he had sent her where he described the battle with the slavers.

The next two days saw Marty dressed in slops and supervising the tarring of the rigging with Stockholm tar. This preserved the cordage from the effects of salt and water but, by god, it was a dirty job and no matter how hard he tried, it got all over him. They were just completing it and he was at the top of the fore mast when he saw a Xebec entering the harbour with a British flag over the French, she had to be the Bouvet!

Sure enough, the Bouvet anchored alongside them and Richard Dicky came across in their ship's boat. Marty sensed something was wrong as soon as Richard's head came up over the side as his expression was unusually solemn. He said nothing but went straight down to the captain's cabin. An hour later, he reappeared and was making his way over to the entry port when he was stopped by Bob Graveny, and Marty overheard him say, "Is it true the Esme was lost in the storm?"

"Aye," replied Richard, "we got separated but when it blew out, we figured they must have been blown along roughly the same course as us, so we tacked back looking for them. All we found was some wreckage with one of our sailors bodies tangled in it."

Marty felt the loss of his friend keenly. Archie had been three years older but had never stinted in helping Marty learn how to derive their position from noon and lunar sightings. He had also started to teach him Latin and a bit of Greek. Their friendship had grown through mutual respect and had been the stronger for it.

The Captain made an announcement to the assembled crew at Sunday service, in which he read a eulogy and the burial at sea in the absence of the lost men.

Richard came back to the Falcon and Midshipman Clegg was sent over with one of the older Bosuns Mates to command the skeleton crew while the Falcon left to find prey in the North.

The Mediterranean was in a contrary mood with shifting winds that were gale force for a few hours, dropping to light breezes and veering to all points of the compass in twenty-four hours. They came out of an overnight storm, where they could hardly see past the end of their own bowsprit into a bright and cheerful dawn and a small fleet of French ships being escorted by a Frigate and a Corvette.

The Falcon reacted fastest as it was standard practice for Navy ships to greet the dawn at quarters in case the dawn revealed an unfriendly sail on the horizon. The Captain steered straight for the lead ship on the windward side. She was the French Frigate Superbe a thirty gunner. They had the weather gauge!

Marty had learnt that having the weather gauge gave one the ability to dictate the battle against another ship and in this case the Captain chose to take them on at the earliest opportunity. They were soon within firing distance of the main guns, and the Captain turned a couple of points to Starboard to bring his broadside to bear. As was the custom amongst Navy ships, they aimed at the other ship's hull "twixt wind and water" to do most damage to her ability to shoot back.

The crash of a full broadside of nine pounders was deafening, and Marty was thankful that he had stuffed his ears with candle wax and tied a cloth around his head as well. He had nothing to do yet as they were a good three cables off their adversary and out of the accurate range of his carronades. As the smoke cleared, he saw that all the practice had paid off as there were numerous star shaped holes along the side of the Superbe. But then, smoke bloomed from her guns, and he felt as much as he heard the scream of bar shot ripping through the rigging above him.

As was their practice, the French had aimed high trying to cripple them. A quick glance aloft told him the damage wasn't too serious. Although there was the upper half of a marine stuck in one of the boarding nets, blood dripping to the deck below and no sign of his lower half. A tap on his shoulder brought him back to deck level and Second Lieutenant Rampole said,

"Captain's complements, and he would be obliged if you could clear their quarterdeck once we get within two cables."

"Aye aye, sir," Marty replied as he hurried to his men to get them to load a murderous charge of twenty-four one-pound grape shot in the larboard carronades and to prepare a reload of canister plus grape for the second helping.

Recently, he had taken to fitting his triple barrelled pepper pot pistols, in their holsters, to his cross belts. He found this better for movement than when he had mounted them on his waist belt. His fighting knife was in the small of his back set for a left-handed draw, and his sword was on his left hip. He was dressed in his silk shirt and stockings with his blood-stained fighting uniform; in all respects, he was ready. He watched the distance reduce between the two ships that were almost abeam. The Falcon let off her second broadside one minute and fifteen seconds after the first.

All of a sudden, there was a hail from the mainmast lookout who had spotted the Corvette approaching rapidly from behind.

Bugger, we might end up the meat in the sandwich, he thought, then realized that the gap was now passing through two cables. Carefully, taking his time, he sighted the first of his guns, aiming between their mizzen and stern rail where he could see the ship's wheel manned by three men with a number of officers stood fairly close together. Satisfied, he stepped back and nodded to his gun captain. CHUFF BOOM, the carronade threw its deadly load out followed rapidly by the second.

Not able to see the result for the smoke, they quickly reloaded. He waited. The smoke thinned until he could see that there was no wheel and come to that there weren't any officers either. He yelled at his men to aim the next two loads at an angle across the deck in front of the Frenchman's quarterdeck so as to clear any crew that might oppose a boarding. The nine pounders barked another broadside.

Before the smoke cleared, he heard a cry from forward, "She's struck," and a huge cheer rippled down the ship from fore to aft. "Silence on deck," bellowed the voice of the First Lieutenant.

"Prepare the Starboard battery."

It was the Corvette, she was closing fast, had the weather gauge on them and if the captain wasn't careful, she would cross his stern and deal them a broadside up the arse.

"Fire as you bear," was the order as the Falcon swung to Starboard across the wind in a frantic wear to prevent being crossed. Marty peered along the barrel of his aft carronade. This time, he was to aim for her rigging with a mixture of case and bar shot. He didn't know it, but the captain planned to disable her and then run alongside to board her. Again, his carronades did their work along with a broadside from the nine pounders and the top half of the Corvette's mainmast collapsed hanging half on the deck and half over the Starboard side.

"BOARDERS PREPARE," came the call. "Carronades one round of cannister to sweep their decks, please." Marty obliged and then led his men to the rail where the two ships met with a resounding thud.

"BOARDERS AWAY," yelled the captain, and his hunting horn sounded the chase.

The men leapt across the gap, screaming and yelling and were met by the French. Marty had a pistol in his left hand and his hanger in his right and found himself face to face with a Frenchman armed with a boarding pike. He fired his pistol at his belly and stepped forward and slashed with his hanger from right to left across his throat. He holstered the gun and reached behind himself for his fighting knife.

Just as he did that, he glimpsed a movement out of the corner of his eye to his left and instinctively ducked. A marlin spike passed over his head and the man wielding it crashed into him, knocking him on to his back on the deck. He looked up to see a large foot heading towards his head in a stamp and he just managed to roll clear in time. He lost his sword, and he groped for his right-hand pistol. Pulling it out and cocking it with his left wrist, he thrust it forward and pulled the trigger. The forty-five-calibre ball hit the Frenchman in the thigh, cutting the femoral artery so that a huge gout of blood spewed forth soaking the deck. Unable to crank the next barrel into line, Marty dropped the gun, switched his knife to his right hand and was about to stab the man through the chest when he sighed and collapsed to the deck. He had bled out that fast.

Just then, a cry went up and the remaining Frenchmen stepped back and started to drop their weapons. They had yielded. This gave Marty time to quickly recover his pistol and sword from the scuppers. He sheathed his blades in preference for his guns as he thought they were better for controlling prisoners. He looked around as he carefully cranked loaded barrels into place and brought them to full cock.

The Forfaite was soon brought totally under the command of the Falcon and the prisoners were herded together on the fore deck covered by a pair of swivels and the Marines. Marty was ordered to stay aboard with Lieutenant Smethers and thirty men as the prize crew while the Falcon went off to take command of the Superbe.

There were still around eighty Frenchmen left on board, so they separated the men from the officers and put them in the hold. The officers were asked to give their parole and if they did, their swords were returned, and they were allowed to stay on deck. Marty reloaded the spent barrels of his pistols and returned them to his cross belts. He didn't trust any Frenchman as far as he could throw them, and he doubted that he could even pick one up!

The deck was a mess. The carronades had done some bloody work, and there were body parts and blood everywhere. So, the first thing he did was to order a deck pump to be rigged. While that was being done, he asked one of the French officers if he spoke English. He shrugged and pointed to a young officer who stood by the mainmast. The young man was probably about fifteen years old and looked to be dressed in the equivalent of a midshipman's uniform. Marty approached and asked,

"Do you speak English?"

The young man looked him up and down, noting the bloody uniform that had obviously seen more than one battle, the weaponry, and the look in Marty's eye.

"Yes, I speak a little," he said, deciding that discretion was the better part of valour. "Can I 'elp you?"

"I am Midshipman Martin Stockley, and you are?" Marty asked politely.

"I am Aspirant Phillippe du Monde," he replied with a slight bow.

"I am pleased to make your acquaintance. I wish it had been under better circumstances, however, I wonder if I could ask if you could place a request to your Captain for me?" Marty asked in his best English.

"I can try. What is it you want?"

"Could you ask him if he would detail off six of your men to man the deck pump? It ain't right that your men's blood still be all over the place." (He couldn't keep it up).

du Monde looked around and winced at the sight as if he was forced to see it for the first time, which he in effect was as he had been studiously not looking at it up to then. This was his first battle and the sight made him feel sick.

"Oui, I will ask 'im," he said.

They walked together over to a short man with no hat, untidy hair, and an ill-fitting uniform. On the way, du Monde said quietly,

"He is a pig. He was a mate on a cargo ship, but he kissed the derriere of the committee and got given this ship. He thinks he is better than he is."

Once they reached him, the aspirant touched his forelock, spoke to the Captain in French, and gestured to the pump and then to Marty. Marty heard the word cochon in his reply and when he finished, he spat on the deck at Marty's feet and turned away. du Monde turned back to Marty, he was obviously angered by what had been said and told him,

"He 'as said that you can do what you want."

"And what were the rest? The bit about a pig?" Marty asked.

"Ah, you know a little French oui? He said, "tell the little pig to go screw 'imself."

If there was one thing Marty couldn't stand, it was people being rude and arrogant, and his temper immediately flared. He stepped right up to the man and said to du Monde,

"Monsieur, please translate exactly if you can."

He poked his finger into the captain's chest and looked him straight in the eye, which wasn't difficult as he was only an inch or so shorter.

"There is only one pig on this ship, and that is you and if you weren't a prisoner, I would call you out and gut you like the pig you are." He then sniffed, making a show of smelling something rank. "And, you stink."

As he turned away, he saw Lieutenant Smethers watching him. He raised one eyebrow as if in query and then both shot up in alarm. Marty heard the sound of a sword being drawn behind him and spun in a half crouch, drawing his hanger at the same time.

The French Captain had his sword raised ready to strike down on him, and as the blow fell, he only just got his blade up in time to parry. He stepped back and went into a fighter's stance. Weight over the balls of his feet, knees slightly bent, balanced to move in any direction as needed.

He reached around behind him with his left hand and drew his fighting Knife as a main gauche. The captain didn't look so sure of himself now but to back down to a junior officer, and a boy at that, would cost him too much pride. So, he did the only other thing he could and attacked.

He was no swordsman, in fact, he fought like a deck hand. He swung the sword like an axe, trying by main strength to beat past Marty's guard, but Marty had been taught all the tricks of fighting that style, so he just parried with his sword angled to divert the blade to the side and stepped back, inviting his opponent to try again.

Again, the Frenchman stepped in and swung his sword in a mighty swing from right to left. This time Marty just swayed back out of range letting the tip of the sword pass him by. He immediately stepped in slamming his sword blade against the captain's just in front of the hilt as it reached the end of its swing, trapping the man's arm across his body. He followed up by thrusting the fighting knife into his side under his ribs puncturing his liver. Then, like the cox had drilled him so many times, he twisted the blade and wrenched it down and across, causing a horrendous wound that finished the fight there and then.

"Mon Dieu!" cried the young aspirant as his captain fell to the deck.

"Damn it, Mr. Stockley, what caused that?" said Lieutenant Smethers, who was approaching from the quarterdeck. He looked down at the stricken man who was bleeding out rapidly on the deck.

"Isn't there enough gore around here without you causing more? You had better have a bloody good explanation as to why a French officer reneged on his parole and attacked you for when the captain reads your report."

"Monsieur! Aspirante du Monde at your service," said du Monde, stepping up and bowing, "I can assure you that Monsieur Stockley is not at fault 'ere and was only defending himself against this dishonourable pig," he looked down at the now dead Captain with a look of absolute disgust.

He really didn't like him! thought Marty.

"Well now, will you bear witness of that to our Captain?" said Smethers.

"Absolutement!" he replied.

"Then carry on, Mr. Stockley, and get this offal off my deck," he said in parting as he returned to the quarterdeck to discuss repairing the main mast with the carpenter's mate as if the whole episode was of no consequence.

"Ice water for blood, that one," said a familiar voice from over his shoulder and when he turned, there was Tom Savage, sword in hand, in range to help out if needed. He bent down and picked up the French Captain's sword.

"I reckon this be yers by right," he said, handing it to Marty. Marty went to take it but realized he still held both his hanger and his knife. He quickly cleaned and sheathed both and took the sword from Tom. It wasn't anything special, and it was too long for his taste, but it was a nice trophy.

Marty called two men over who had stopped work to watch the fight and asked them to move the corpse over to the row of dead that would be buried that evening after the ship was made seaworthy. They grabbed a foot each and were about to move it when du Monde stopped them. He bent over the body and took off the sword belt and scabbard. He held out his hand to Marty for the sword and slid it into the scabbard. Then to Marty's surprise, he reached around Marty's waist and buckled the belt on so it hung just behind his own sword. The men grinned and dragged the body across the deck, leaving a bloody smear in their wake and dumped it at the end of the row.

"Cover it! Don't just leave it there," Marty called, recovering his wits as they were about to walk away.

"Who is the senior officer now?" Marty asked.

"He is," du Monde said, indicating the young man he had spoken to first. "He was the Enseigne de vaisseau. He is the only one left apart from me."

They approached him, and du Monde repeated the request for men, which was approved with a vigorous nodding of the head and even a little bow.

"I sink you 'ave made an impression on 'im," chuckled du Monde.

Six men were called up from the hold by du Monde while Marty and two Marines stood watch, weapons ready. But there was no trouble, and the men took their place at the pump and started work without comment. His men then used swabs to rinse as much blood and offal from the deck and anywhere else it had splashed onto as they could. Once that was done, and they could all walk without slipping once again, Marty had the French seamen returned to the hold, after he thanked them, and detailed his men off to repair rigging.

That evening, the mast repair crew was getting ready to hoist a spare main spar borrowed from the Falcon up to replace the missing part of the main mast. Marty stood by the mizzen with du Monde.

"I must thank you for your support with our lieutenant," he said and held out his hand.

du Monde took it in a firm grip and said, "You are most welcome. You did me a favour killing that pig monsieur."

"My name is Martin or Marty, if you like," said Marty still holding his hand.

"Then you may call me Phillippe," laughed du Monde and they shook once again.

"Tell me about yourself," Marty asked.

"Mon papa is, or was, a junior member of the aristocracy and when the revolution 'appened, he made sure he was always useful to the committee. It was not the most pleasant of times and certainly not honourable, but he knew that to survive the terror he 'ad to do what he 'ad to do."

He sighed and looked out to sea, "He 'ad to bear witness against some of his friends, but if he 'ad not then the whole family would have been sent to Madam Guillotine. Anyway, we survived, and now he is a Secretary to the under commissionaire for the Navy, which is 'ow I got to be an aspirante."

"And how come you speak good English?"

"That is the biggest of my family's secrets," he laughed.

"My maternal grandmother was English, and she taught me 'ow to speak it. She came from a place called York. Where do you come from?"

"I come from a place called Furzebrook in the county of Dorset. That be on the South coast, West of Portsmouth. My family be clay miners and have been for ever as far as I know."

"You are not an aristocrat?" Serge asked in surprise. "I was led to believe that all British officers were aristos or from wealthy families."

"Not all, although it is certain that there are a lot in the service." replied Marty.

"I was a servant and ship's boy until I had the good fortune to help the daughter of the Count de Marchets and earn his favour. It was his interest in me, after that, which got me a midshipman's berth."

"The Conte de Marchets?" cried Phillippe. "Why I know him and his family. They are wanted by the committee for crimes against the state!"

"Well, they be safe now in England," Marty said, looking warily at his new friend.

"Oh, that is good news," said Serge. "He was a grand gentleman, and his family were always good to the people that worked their estates. How did you meet them?"

Marty really had no choice but to recount his adventures in Toulon. He left out the details of his fights and kept it to the general story.

"Mon dieu," said Serge after the story. "So, the Conte has sponsored you. That is magnifique."

"Why don't you join him in England?" Marty asked.

"Alas, that I cannot do," he replied. "If I did, my family would be put to the Guillotine. I am trapped and must make the best of it."

Just then, a cheer went up and Marty saw that the jury-rigged mast was in position and a spar had been hauled up.

"I must go, we will be making sail soon," he said.

There was a signal from the Falcon for all Captains to report aboard and Smethers had himself rowed over. He returned a short time later with written orders and called Marty to him on the quarterdeck.

"We are to take the prize in convoy with the Falcon and Superbe to Mahon where we will collect the Bouvet and then sail on to Gibraltar. But first, we will sail across to the Spanish/French border and send the prisoners ashore. We don't have enough men to guard them all the way to Gibraltar. This fine ship is ours, Martin, until we hand her over to the prize court!" the two of them grinned at each other.

"I reported the incident with the French Captain to Captain Turner, and he would like a full written report with a signed statement from that French mid. He thinks that no fault lies with you, so do not worry. Now, I will organize three watches with the Bosun's mate taking the third. If you would take the foremast watch, I will take the mainmast, and the mate can take the mizzen." This gave them ten men per watch and maximized the time the men could rest in between. All hands would be called for sail setting and trimming, but in between, ten men should be enough once the prisoners were put ashore.

After Marty told him he would be put ashore, du Monde approached him on his watch and said, "Martin, can I 'ave a moment?" Getting a nod in reply, he continued. "There are several men of my crew that are not 'appy serving the revolution. Three are French, and I sink that their loyalties are with the Bourbons, the rest are Basques. If you call for volunteers to stay and sign wis the British Navy, I sink those seven will step forward. Please do not metion zat I 'ave spoken for zem, or it will cost me my 'ead." Marty noted that his accent had got much more French and thought that a good indication he was under some level of stress.

"Thank you for bringing it to my attention, Phillippe. I will talk to the lieutenant and don't worry, I will keep it close," Phillippe smiled, nodded, and hurriedly left the quarterdeck.

Around the end of his watch, they hove to off a little fishing village called Cerbére. There was a sheltered bay with a headland sticking out at the Southern end. The boats were lowered, and they could see that the Superbe was starting to off load their prisoners. Marty had talked to Smethers who had agreed to let him have a try at recruiting the dissatisfied prisoners.

He had asked Phillipe if he could make a written statement about the fight with his Captain and to write down in French the request for volunteers. Now, armed with both those papers he stood in front of the first twenty prisoners that had been let up from the hold under a watchful armed guard and covered by swivels.

He coughed and then reading carefully, he asked the question. No one stepped forward. So, he asked it again, this time holding up a silver guinea. Again, no one moved. So, he sent the men down, ten to a boat, with Marines stationed fore and aft to ensure there were no last-minute heroics.

The next twenty were brought up. He asked the question and this time four men stepped forward. He immediately saw that they looked different than the rest with darker complexions and harder faces. *The Basques,* he thought. He indicated that they step over to where Smethers had set up a table with paper and pen ready. As they had pre-arranged, Smethers made a show of asking their names and getting them to make their mark. He then ostentatiously handed each man a silver florin. This was more than the regular 'king's shilling' but these were extraordinary circumstances. Another man, a tall blond, stood forward and asked in singsong accented English,

"Do ya British pay yor sailors?"

"Aye, a florin to join and ten pound a year, plus prize money," Marty said, indicating the ship around them.

"I'm with you den," the blond replied and stepped over to the table. Turned out he was Danish and was called Pedersen. Marty wondered how he ended up in the French Navy, he would ask him later.

The remaining men were sent ashore once the boats had returned and the next twenty called up. He went through the routine again. Nobody stepped forward.

One last time, he asked the question to the last group. There was a long pause, and then three men pushed their way forward. Several of the other men made to pull them back, but Marty pulled a pistol and fired a shot over their heads. That restored order. He didn't know it but the story of his fight with the French Captain had been told and retold amongst the prisoners and with each telling, he had been painted as a being more bloodthirsty until he held an almost demonic status.

"AVAST THAT," he shouted and once the three were clear, he beckoned them forward.

"Get the rest into the boats now!" he ordered to forestall any chance of retribution on what they must have seen as traitors. Finally, they boarded the two officers. Marty stopped them both at the entry port and shook their hands then stepped back and saluted. They returned the salute and climbed down into the boat.

The next few days passed fairly peacefully as they worked their way back South to Mahon against a contrary breeze. The new hands were distributed amongst the watches and he found himself with the Dane, Peter Pedersen, two of the Basques, Pablo Esquibel and Antton Elkano and one of the French, Roland du Demaine. Where Pedersen was tall and blond, du Demaine had short legs and a stocky body, dark, close-curled hair, and dark eyes. The two Basques were almost twins. Dark hair tied back with a bandana, dark brown eyes, tanned skin.

Tom Savage took them under his wing and started teaching them English and the English names for the ropes, tackles, sails and so on.

Pedersen was twenty years old, a gunner and had to leave Denmark in a hurry after having an affair with a nobleman's wife. The nobleman had caught them in flagrante delicto and had made a serious attempt to castrate him. He had to leave town, as after he escaped the nobleman's clutches, the cuckolded man put a bounty on his head. The quickest way out of town was to sign up with the French Naval ship that was in Copenhagen harbour at that time. He had been in the Navy ever since, which was now around two years. He'd learnt gunnery in that time but was never really happy, and the revolutionary government was notorious for not paying their sailors what they were due. He helped to teach the others English and acted as translator as he spoke Danish, French, and English fluently.

Pablo and Antton were both Basques from the Northern part of the region. They, with their two mates, had gone to sea as fishermen and had fought in the war of the Pyrenees where they ended up being rounded up by the French and given the choice of the Guillotine or the Navy. They told that large numbers of Basques were being forcibly conscripted into the French Army and Navy. They had a hatred for the French that surprised Marty until he realized that it stemmed from the absorption of their homeland into the French state and the French attempts to eradicate their national identity.

du Demaine was a surprise. He was quick and intelligent, and it turned out, a surprisingly good cook. His ancestry had some Algerian in it, hence the tight curls. He was quick with a knife, and Marty took advantage to practice his knife fighting with him in his off hours. Once Smethers found out about his cooking skills, he was made ship's cook almost immediately as the hand that had been given the job couldn't cook water without burning it.

When they finally got to Mahon, they found the Bouvet just where they had left her. The mathematics of manning three large prizes struck home; one hundred men were all that were left manning the Falcon now as thirty were on the Forfaite and sixty on the Superbe, commanded by Lieutenant Gentry with Midshipman Mulhoon. Graveny replaced Clegg in charge of a prize crew of ten on the Bouvet. If they had to fight, they would be seriously undermanned on every ship. On top of that, their officers were spread as thin as honey on hot toast.

The captain called a conference, which left Marty in command on the Forfaite. He had felt a little strange the last few weeks. He had been growing fast and was rapidly running out of room in his uniform. He also noticed changes in his body, especially around the groin. He had woken up with an erection, which scared him the first time it happened, and his dreams had turned erotic. He was also getting hairy around 'there' and under his arms. Then, as he was calling orders to some men on the foredeck, his voice suddenly shifted from alto to tenor and back again. Worse, he started getting pimples on his face, on his back, everywhere! He went to see Tom and confided in him. Tom smiled and told him not to worry about it as what he was experiencing was a natural part of growing up and was when a boy turned in to a man. He also told him to watch his temper as boys going through the change often got overly aggressive.

"Well, how long will this last?" he asked.

"Until you are around sixteen or seventeen," Tom replied.

"Damn," Marty sighed.

Chapter 10: The Last Leg

Smethers returned. "We sail on the morning tide," he told them. "We are as ready as we are going to be, so make sure the men stay sharp. We are going to need luck as well as skill to get to Gibraltar and not meet any Frenchie's. Orders are to scatter and run if signalled by the captain."

He showed Marty an envelope. "These are the written orders. I will store them in the desk in my cabin and if anything happens to me, you are to obey them to the letter. Understood? Go to the Spirit room, make sure it's locked and post a guard. One thing we don't need is drunk hands."

"Aye Aye, sir," Marty replied.

He was off watch when they sailed. He had the 04:00 to 08:00 watch that morning, so he had the luxury of being an interested observer. The Falcon raised the signals 'prepare to sail' then 'make sail' and as the flags were dropped in the execute, all four ships came up to their anchors, the sails dropped and caught the wind that was, fortuitously, blowing gently down the channel. Once out to sea, the Superbe led, followed by the Bouvet, then the Forfaite. The Falcon positioned herself to the windward side of the little squadron so she could sail down in support of any that were attacked.

The Forfaite was an older Corvette with sixteen six-pound guns on her single deck. She was about ninety feet long. The thirty-eight strong complement would be able to fire a one-sided broadside as long as they didn't need to change or trim the sails or they could put just three men to a gun leaving fourteen men to steer and sail, but their rate of fire would be really slow.

As they had a fair wind and didn't need to keep changing the set of the sails, Smethers had Marty practice both scenarios, running out the guns, miming firing and reloading. With four men to a gun, they could just about manage a round every one and a half minutes, but with only three men, that dropped to a minute forty five seconds. Looking forward, he could see that the Bouvet was doing a similar exercise with her four pounders. He assumed that the Superbe would be doing the same with their nines.

He decided to inspect the ship's magazine, so he rounded up Pedersen and took him down below with him. When they got there, they first donned felt slippers and left every metal article outside. They entered and were surprised to find very few pre-made cartridges for either the deck guns or the swivels.

There were enough empty bags made up for two broadsides and plenty of powder. However, when he looked closely, he saw it was grainier than the English powder that he was used to on the Falcon and not as consistently ground. When he mentioned that to Pedersen, the man just shrugged and said it was the normal quality on French ships and it didn't burn consistently either. He left Pedersen with orders to fill all the available cartridge bags for the main guns and as many as he could find for the swivels. He returned to the main deck and found Tom.

"Who of the crew can sew up cartridge bags, Tom?"

"I think John Smith and Willy Carter be the ones who did it most of this crew." Tom replied.

Marty had seen John Smith on his way to find Tom, so he went to him and, on his way, spotted Willy loitering in the waste. He gathered them up and sent them below to Pedersen with instructions to make up another three broadsides of cartridge bags. Then he had a realization, "there aren't any boys on this ship! DAMN!"

He immediately went to Smethers.

"Sir, we have a problem," he started.

Smethers raised an eyebrow in enquiry.

"We have just enough men for a broadside," he continued, "but we don't have any ship's boys to bring up the cartridge."

Smethers looked thoughtful for a moment.

"If we get into a situation where we are going to have to fight our way out, it will be desperate enough that we will take the risk of stowing spare cartridge on the centreline behind the guns for," he paused and thought some more, "three broadsides. At our rate of fire, that's all we will get away before we are boarded."

Things took a turn for the worst that evening. Dark, angry-looking clouds were seen boiling up, and the wind began to veer to the East as they approached. Thompson, the acting master's mate, sniffed the air and pronounced that they were in for a blow.

Really? thought Marty sarcastically, I *would have never guessed.*

"Falcon's signalling," shouted the lookout.

Marty swarmed up the ratlines to get a better view with a small telescope he had found in the First Lieutenant's cabin that he now occupied. He read it and shouted down, "All ships reduce sail," as he jumped down to the signal cupboard and got out the correct flags to acknowledge the signal. Being the last ship in the convoy, they were careful to maintain their cable length separation from the Bouvet. Smethers joked that, "running them up the arse with our Bowsprit won't win us any prizes with the captain."

They asked the cook if there was a chance of an early dinner. "Mon dieu! que pensez-vous que je suis un faiseur de miracles?" he all but shouted angrily.

Marty just took him by the arm, led him up onto deck, and pointed at the approaching storm.

"Alors!" he cried and disappeared below, calling out for Anton Bressy, one of the other.

Dinner was served up an hour later. He had worked wonders with salt beef that had been soaked for God knows how long and then stewed with onions, dried peas, and some carrots they had got in Mahon. It was beautifully seasoned with some herbs and was delicious. He had even made dumplings instead of potatoes to go with it.

The storm caught up with them around two in the morning and the entire crew had very little sleep as they were constantly reefing and trimming the sails. They had to man the pumps for four hours as well as it turned out that the Forfaite was a damp ship in a blow.

The good thing was the storm passed relatively quickly after a mere nine hours and, when it did, the wind dropped, and the sun burst through the clouds. The bad thing was they found themselves all alone on the sea.

They guessed they had been blown well to the North as the winds had veered from East to South over the course of the storm. Noon saw a break in the cloud that had become scattered, allowing them to take a sighting. They figured they were somewhere just South of Ibiza.

Smethers got them back on the course that the captain had plotted figuring that the others would do the same and they would all congregate around Cartagena. They were making a good six knots under moderate sail and should be there around two o'clock the following afternoon.

At around 11am, the lookout reported he could hear gunfire to the South. A half hour later, he reported that he could see sails to the South, Southeast. Marty was sent aloft with a 'bring 'em near' to see if he could see what was going on. He scaled the foremast to the topsail yard, made himself comfortable, and got the big telescope up to his eye. He first scanned the horizon slowly from East to West and then slowly back again until he saw the unmistakable shape of a topsail. Steadying the telescope, he focused in and could see smoke drifting away from it. He bided his time and soon a second topmast came into view. He recognized the second immediately. It was the Falcon!

"Deck there!" he cried. "The Falcon is hull down South by Southeast of us, and she is engaged with a French frigate."

"Thank you, Mr. Stockley" called Smethers.

"Come down now, if you please." Marty obliged by making use of a stay and descending hand over hand as fast as he could. A new lookout was sent up and instructed to call down regular updates.

"Well, what do you think?" asked Smethers when Marty arrived on the quarterdeck.

"Hard to tell exactly, sir. But my guess is that they be evenly matched, despite the shortage of men on the Falcon and with the Falcon having the weather gauge they are avoiding getting boarded forcing the Frenchy into a pounding match"

Smethers thought for a good minute or so and then said, "Then we may tip the balance if we can get there in time. Make all sail and get as much speed out of this bitch as we can. Then raise the signal 'Enemy in sight'."

They piled on as much canvas as the jury-rigged ship would bear and got the speed up to eight knots and a fathom. But even then, they knew it would take almost an hour and a half to travel the twelve or so miles to the fight. Smethers cleared for action after forty minutes. The decks were wetted and sanded, and Marty had four broadsides worth of cartridge brought up from the magazine. Ten minutes later they could see both ships from the deck. The Falcon had lost her main topmast and the foremast didn't look particularly safe. The French ship had taken a battering as well but looked to be trying to get alongside to board.

Smethers called Marty over. "Run up a set of French colours then get the Starboard guns loaded with double shot. If we are lucky, he will think we are coming to his aid until we get right up to him. Once we show our true colours, I'm going to run across his stern, and I want you to make every shot count. Then I will wear, and we will repeat the exercise with the larboard guns."

"Aye, Aye, sir," warbled Marty, whose voice chose that moment to break.

They reduced sail to just topsails as they approached to a couple of cables and swapped to their own colours. They were only travelling at walking speed when they swung across the Frenchman's stern a scant cable away. Marty wondered why they hadn't opened up on them but quickly put the thought aside as the stern was approaching. He was at the first gun and looking down the barrel as the centre of the transom came into view. "Fire!" he told the gun captain and jumped aside as the sailor placed the linstock to the touch hole. He didn't wait or look back as the gun banged. He was at the second gun, yelled fire, and moved down all eight of them.

"Load and run out the Larboard guns," he yelled, pushing the men from the last gun across to the other side of the ship.

"Only three per gun," he thought as one man from each gun was helping wear ship. The ship came around slowly, so they were easily in time for their second pass. This time Marty noticed the damage they had done. The transom was peppered with shot holes and he knew that those shot had careened down the open gun deck with nothing to stop them causing death and destruction in their passing. The only thing that had opposed them was some musket fire from her tops.

Time for your second dose of medicine, he thought as he sighted the first gun. The broadside rolled from bow to stern.

"Ready the Starboard guns," he yelled as they cleared the Paris's stern for the second time. Marty had spotted her name in Gold letters across her stern. But then a shout went up,

"She's on fire!"

Marty rushed across the deck and climbed up the mizzen rat lines for a better view and sure enough, smoke was boiling up from below decks. Fire was every sailor's worst nightmare. Wooden ships were coated in stuff that burned really well and any fire could quickly take over and destroy a wooden warship in minutes.

"Steer us clear!" ordered Smethers to the Quartermaster as a plume of flame erupted from amidships of the stricken Frigate. Marty could see that the Falcon was also desperately trying to distance herself from the flames.

Smethers had joined him at the stern and said,

"they must abandon her soon," when there was an almighty explosion, and the Paris disappeared in a cloud of smoke and debris was hurled in all directions.

"Bugger me, but her magazine has gone up," said Smethers as they poked their heads above the rail after literally hitting the deck instinctively. They could see the Falcon in the distance, men on her decks frantically putting out small fires caused by falling debris. They looked around at their own ship and saw, with relief, that they had missed the worst of it and that they weren't any fires.

They did a quick round of the ship, looking for casualties and were happy to only find one. A topman called Winston had been winged with a musket ball and had a flesh wound on his shoulder. They saw to it that a clean strip of cloth was wrapped around it after pouring neat brandy on it. The swearing that issued forth from Winston when the neat spirit hit the open wound was a wonder. Marty would swear afterwards he didn't repeat himself for a full minute if not two.

They wore ship and made their way to the Falcon. When they were within hailing distance, Smethers called across and asked if they could be of assistance. The captain appeared at the rail and said, "We are fine, we have some casualties and need to make repairs, but are still swimming. Make a search for survivors and thank you for your timely intervention!"

They hove to and lowered their boats and almost immediately hoisted one of them back on board when they found that there was a bullet hole through the side below the waterline. The second boat with the Bosun's mate in command started a search of the floating debris.

"Sail ho!" they heard echo across the water from the Falcon. "Where away?" someone asked.

"Three points off the Starboard quarter. Looks like a Xebec in company with a French Frigate."

"I hope that's the Superbe and the Bouvet," Marty said to Smethers.

"I don't think we can stand up to another attack right now," he added, nodding towards the Falcon, who ran up the recognition signal. Apparently, they got an acceptable reply as the signal came down and everyone looked relaxed.

Sometime later, a boat came across from the Falcon with Midshipman Clegg on board. He looked to have his sea chest with him. Once he got aboard, he handed over an envelope to Smethers. He didn't look very happy, and Marty was wondering what was up.

"Martin," called Smethers.

Bugger, I must be in trouble if he's using my first name, thought Marty

"It would appear that Lieutenant Dicky has been wounded and is unable to do his duties. You are to return to the Falcon and Mr. Clegg will take your place here. The captain has also called an all officers conference, so I will accompany you over."

Marty went below and quickly threw his things into his sea chest then, with the help of a crewman, hauled it up on deck. He was surprised to see six men standing by the entry way with their sea bags, grins on their faces. Tom Savage, John Smith the fifth, and the four Basques.

Smethers walked over and inclined his head.

"The captain also requested we send back six men, so I asked for volunteers and it seems that after a discussion amongst the crew that these were the only six. I want to thank you, Martin. You have made running this ship easy for me."

He chuckled, and with a glance at Midshipman Clegg, added, "I have a feeling it's about to get harder."

The captain welcomed him back aboard and immediately opened the meeting.

"Gentlemen, welcome back. Our unfortunate encounter with the Paris had a pleasant side effect in that the sound of the explosion and the smoke acted as a beacon for our stray lambs to return to the fold. Now to the present, we will be making sail as soon as possible, as that which acted as a beacon for our own could also have got the attention of our enemies. Mr. Smethers, did you find any survivors?"

"Just two, sir," replied Smethers, "both jumped overboard before the explosion. Our new Danish gunner questioned them, and it seems that when we sent the first broadside up her stern it smashed a lanthorn that had been left lit. The burning oil caught fire to the usual rubbish the French leave all over their decks and the fire soon spread and got out of hand. We also asked them if they damped down the felt doors to the magazine and they didn't know what we were talking about. Our conclusion is that the fire just flashed down into the magazine and, well, BOOM"

"Thank you, I assume that will all be in your written report?"

"Aye, sir."

"Now," the captain continued, "My plan is to make all possible speed for Gibraltar in convoy for mutual protection. We will change the formation. Falcon will wear French colours over our own to make her look like the prize. The other three will show French colours. Forfait will lead, followed by Bouvet, and Falcon will bring up the rear. Superbe will take the Weather gauge and behave like the escort. Is that clear so far?"

They all nodded or Aye Aye'd.

"We captured a French signal book, I have had it copied and you will all get one, so we know what the recognition signal is for this month. Now, if we are attacked by a single ship, up to and including a Frigate, who isn't taken in by that and is foolish enough to attack on their own we will fight as follows. Bouvet will pull out of the line and generally get out of the way as she doesn't carry enough firepower to make a difference."

Graveny had a sour look on his face but nodded.

"Superbe will engage the enemy and hold them until Falcon and Forfait can join in. We will try and bracket them with the frigates and Forfait can attempt to get across their bows or stern and rake them. If they strike, we will work out how to include them as a prize, otherwise we sink them. However, if we are faced with more than one adversary, we run like a fox pursued by the hunt. If they get too close, we scatter. I will signal that with a double gun and one over nine from both the mizzen and the foremasts. You will all be responsible for make your own way to Gibraltar. Is everything clear?"

There were Aye Ayes all around. "Now a toast. Confusion to the French!"

"Confusion to the French!" they all cried and drained their glasses.

"Now on your way. God speed and good luck!"

They all started to leave when the captain said,

"Mr. Rampole and Mr. Stockley, please stay for a moment."

Marty and the second lieutenant glanced at each other and returned to stand in front of the captain's desk. He looked at each in turn.

"We are down to a scant eighty-five men after that fight and twenty of them are walking wounded. Add to that the six you brought back with you from the Forfate, Mr. Stockley and we have ninety-one if they are able."

He looked at Marty who replied, "Tom Savage and John Smith the fifth are our own and unhurt. The other four are Basques and are experienced top men but their English is limited to simple instructions, and they need to be aided by gestures. We put them with Tom on the Forfate and they just followed his lead."

"So, you would recommend that we keep those six together?"

"Aye sir, I would."

"You two are the only two officers I have now that Mr. Dicky got himself shot. The surgeon says he will recover as long as he stays clear of infection but will need total rest for at least a month before he can even get out of his hammock. We will run a three-watch system. I will take the Foremast, Mr. Rampole the Main, and Mr. Stockley, you will take the Mizzen. My standing orders are that you call me if there is any change in the weather or a ship is sited. Am I clear?"

They both nodded. He passed Marty a small book.

"Here are my standing orders. Read and memorize them. Now, let's get under way, we can continue the repairs as we go."

The captain had the watch, but Marty was still busy overseeing repairs. Any shot holes below the waterline had already been repaired but there was substantial damage to the upper works that need to be attended to. They were sailing with a foreshortened foremast and that was the main priority. Marty spoke to the carpenter, and he told them they had gotten a spare mainmast spar from the Superbe and were fashioning a new top half to the foremast which they would fish on in the morning. That would mean bringing the convoy to a halt while the repair was made but if they started at first light, it could be finished by midday. Other repairs were underway to rigging and around the deck area and he found his six ex-Forfait's helping the sailmaker.

"All well, Tom?" he asked, "Aye, sir," Tom replied.

Be dammed if I'm ever going to get used to that! he thought.

"How are our friends here getting on?" he asked.

"They be doing all right. They be fair hands and ready to do any job. Fast learners too, well three of them be. Paulo as a bit of trouble with learning English but we'm getting there. He follows John there around like a puppy and they seem to be communin' well enough."

The weather picked up a bit over night with a nasty short chop that made the ship spiral in an uncomfortable fashion, which was made worse by the foreshortened foresail and stayed with them during the next morning. The good thing was it hurried them along and they were somewhere off the gulf of Almeria, when just after midday the wind dropped, allowing them to heave to so the Falcon could raise the Jury-rigged foremast. They were just hauling it up when the mainmast lookout called "Sail Ho! three points off the larboard bow."

Rampole was supervising the mast repair, so Marty was sent up the mast to see if he could see what it was. Up he went, hanging out at forty-five degrees as he went around the futtock shrouds and up into the tops. He did a sweep with his telescope first and then homed in on the spec of sail the lookout had spotted. It had lateen sails on the fore, he could just make out the top of it, but he couldn't make out anything else. It was obviously sailing close to the wind and didn't look to have spotted them yet. He reported what he could see and waited. Twenty minutes later, he could see she was a Xebec. She had lateen sails on the fore, square on the main and he judged that she was bigger than the Bouvet. The masts came in to line. She had turned towards them.

He used a stay to get down to the deck fast and went to the captain to report. "Could you see her colours?" asked the captain.

"No sir. She be sailin' straight at us and I couldn't see 'em," Marty replied.

"If only we had a French speaker on board," said the captain, "we might be able to bluff her if she is French."

"Sir, there be the Dane on the Forfait. He speaks French and English and there be the three Frenchie's as well. If we get him over with one of them would that do it? Nobody would believe the Basques were officers if that is what yer 'ad in mind, sir."

"Hmm, that might work. We need to get the crew looking French as well. You go get the Dane and a Frenchman. I will see to the rest. Oh, and pass the word to the other ships what we will do. We have about three hours before he beats his way up to us."

Marty took the Gig and went to the Forfait. He boarded and told Smethers what was planned. Clegg was sent to find Pedersen and the Frenchmen, Reynard. He was acting as assistant cook to du Demaine and was the one they would miss least. When the two men showed up with their sea bags, Clegg was given the task of rowing over to the other ships to spread the plan.

Once aboard, they dressed Reynard in a mishmash of cloths that made him look like a somewhat scruffy French junior officer who had been put in charge of a prize crew. The Captain planned that most of the crew would be hidden below decks only leaving the 'prize crew' on deck finishing off the repair to the mast. In case things should not go as planned, the guns would be loaded but not run out. Marty was dressed in slops and loitered near the mainmast if they were forced to react to the Xebec, then he would be ready.

The lookout called down, "I can see his colours, sir. He be Spanish."

The captain wasn't convinced, "Stay alert he may be playing the same game as us. If he is French, he will change his colours as soon as he is sure who we are."

The Xebec, however, veered away as soon as they saw that all four ships were flying French colours. He was indeed a Spaniard.

The captain said, "We will let him think he escaped a French squadron. Stand the men down."

Repairs were completed, and they got back under way starting the long leg West by Southwest toward Gibraltar. The wind was predominantly from the Northwest which made progress slow and would make entering the bay of Gibraltar almost impossible. However, two days later, the wind started to veer around to the North and then Northeast as the barometer rose. They met a couple of British ships who told them that this part of the Mediterranean was still firmly under British control and felt comfortable to proceed under their real colours.

They got a real scare, when a squadron of four Spanish ships, made up of two Liners of seventy-five guns, a Frigate, and the armed Xebec they had seen earlier bore down on them from the Northeast with the apparent intent of engaging them. The fact that they were showing British colours didn't seem to convince the Spanish Commodore as he kept coming with his ports open and guns run out!

They made their number and the day's recognition signal but got no answer other than a shot from the leading ship's fore chasers. So, the Captain ordered the colours struck. The Liners could blow them to matchwood in no time and he didn't want the "excitable gentleman in charge over there" to make a mistake.

They were boarded and the captain was taken over to the lead ship, that had a Commodores pennant flying, along with Lieutenant Rampole. That left Marty in charge. After two hours he was beginning to worry, after three, he was starting to sweat and not just from the heat as the sun had come out and the temperature was rapidly rising.

The Spanish had run their guns in about ten minutes after the captain had boarded but their ports were still open. Almost four hours after they had left, a boat was spotted rounding the bow of the Spanish ship and they could see their officers seated in the stern.

As soon as they appeared on the deck, it was obvious that they were both exceedingly drunk!

"Mishter Shtockley, would you be sho kind as to get ush underway," slurred the captain, "I am going below." And he made his way aft escorted by his cox. Mr. Rumpole winked at Marty and said, "Those Shpanierds inshisted we stay for lunch and they keep a wonderful sheller." He hiccupped and staggered off towards his own quarters. Marty was astonished but managed to pull himself together. He called the two nearest bosuns mates to him.

"Captain wants us under way," he said.

"You know the drill. Let's get the foresail pulling and then set the mains."

He waited, expecting one of the experienced men to tell him he was wrong but they both just nodded and turning to the men started yelling orders. With a start, Marty remembered he had to tell the other ships to get moving too and ran to the signal locker and raised a preparatory with make sail signal. He then detailed a hand to man the halyard and ran up to the quarterdeck where he was greeted by a grinning quartermaster.

He looked aft to the other ships and saw they had raised the acknowledge. He yelled, "Execute!" and the hand lowered the signal. The quartermaster reported, "Rudder's answering, Sur," and "Steering South by Southwest." He just remembered to dip their colours in salute to the Spanish as they drew away.

Esi came up on to the quarterdeck and offered him a cup of coffee. "Cap'ain's going to have to sleep for a bit. He said them Spanish must av poured half a dozen bottles down 'im."

"Christ, Esi, I cain't run the Falcon on me own! What if we sees a Frenchie?" Marty practically sobbed.

"Stiffen up boy!" Esi hissed in a whisper.

"You need to make the 'ands fink you know what you be at or they will start fretting. You got to keep this ship under control and that's a fact. I will go down to the wardroom and me and Thomas will pour coffee down Rampole's throat until he do sober up so he can relieve you."

"Thanks, Esi," Marty said and squaring his shoulders, he took command.

They entered the port of Gibraltar on the tenth of April just under three months after they left. Apart from thanking him for getting them underway, the incident was never mentioned again, even though Marty had command of the Falcon for a full watch until Rampole was sober enough to relieve him. As they entered the harbour and gave their salute to the Flagship, there was already a signal with their number for the captain to report aboard. As they anchored, the captain's barge was pulled around and manned with Marty in command and the Cox at the rudder. He wore his best uniform, and all the sailors were dressed in their matching outfits and freshly shaved. All in all, they looked most presentable.

Chapter 11: A Short Rest

The captain returned and told them that they had been ordered to report to the yard for repair and once they were in all respects ready to sail, they were to return to patrol the area between the Balearic Islands and Toulon. Not all of the French fleet had been destroyed and the admiral wanted a ship in the region to keep an eye on them.

He agreed to buy in the Superbe and Forfait but he would leave it to the prize court to dispose of the Bouvet. The good news was the prize money would be substantial and they would get head money for the Frigate that was destroyed as well. Life had definitely changed for the better.

With a full crew back on board, they warped the Falcon into the Navy yard and waited for their new foremast and other repairs. While she was there, the crew were granted shore leave by watches. They had been issued tickets on their back pay and many redeemed them with the scrimps who infested every port at ten shillings to the pound. Marty left his pay where it was and went to the local branch of Coutts bank where he drew five pounds. He needed to replace the ruined uniform and get his other one let out so it would last another trip.

While he was there, Mr. Spinner, the representative for the bank, recommended a prize agent, a Mr. Crabshaw, as he would be due a tidy sum from the prizes they had brought in. He also recommended that he invest it in the four percents as that would give him a guaranteed income without impacting his capital.

He gave Marty a letter of introduction, so he visited said Mr. Crabshaw and handed it over. Mr. Crabshaw looked him up and down and asked which ship he was from. When he was told the Falcon, he informed Marty that he was also acting for Captain Turner while Gibraltar was their base, and that he already had an estimate of the overall prize money due from their recent successful cruise. He checked a paper from a stack on his desk and then worked out some numbers on an abacus. His share he was informed was likely to be in the order of four and a half thousand pounds (that being an eighth of the eighth for mids, surgeon's mates, and captain's clerk) for just the Frigate and Corvette. He would probably be due another few hundred from the sale of the Xebec and head money. He was bloody rich!

He wrote letters to his family, Miss Turner, and of course, Evelyn. He told them all about the battles, the death of Archie and how much he missed him. He didn't tell his family how much prize money he had won but he did ask Miss Turner to please help his family manage their half of his pay as he had visions of his father trying to drink the money away.

The work at the yard was slow. It seemed that, like Navy dockyards everywhere, a large amount of grease had to be applied to the gears in the form of bribes to get anything done. Since they had been so successful, those bribes were proportionately large. Marty thought this was disgraceful but when he expressed his opinion in the hearing of the captain, he was told that this was the way it had always been and was how it always would be.

Unexpectedly, he was called to the captain's cabin. When he was announced and entered, he saw that Esi and the cox were also there. The captain asked him to sit down as he had some bad news for him.

"Marty, I have had a letter from my sister, Kate. She has informed me that there was a collapse at the mine your father and brothers were working at, and I am sorry to tell you that your father and brother Thomas were badly injured."

Marty made to ask a question, but the captain held up his hand and continued. "Your father's back was broken and although he is alive, he cannot walk. Your brother, I am afraid, died a short time after the accident."

"How be my mother and the rest managing?" Marty asked after taking a deep breath to steady himself.

"My sister tells me that your older siblings are helping as much as they can and that the money you are sending will keep them comfortably as long as they keep the house."

Marty thought for a second or two, putting aside his grief.

"You know I have an account at Coutts, sir?"

"Yes, I am aware of that."

"I 'ave been an signed up with Mr. Crabshaw the prize agent too. He be telling me I 'ave some prize money comin'."

"I think I know where you are heading with this," Captain Turner interposed. "You wish to send some extra money to your family?" He noted that Marty had reverted to his home dialect under the stress.

"Well sort of, sir," Marty replied, "I was thinkin' more of like," he paused as he gathered his thoughts and sorted out the idea that was forming in his head.

"Well I am thinking that they'm never gonna be able to manage a lot o' money. Dad would just drink it or some bugger would come and take it from 'em. What I'm thinking is that they get some money every week to pay for what they need from somfin like the four percent."

The captain pondered for a few moments and then asked, "You want to set up a fund and use the interest to help your family?"

"Ay, that kind of thing," he said.

"We will go to Coutts tomorrow morning and see what can be done. Now, please have the rest of the day to yourself. John and Esi are here for you if you need someone to talk to."

"Thankee, sir," Marty said and stood. It was then that the shock finally hit him, and he lurched towards Esi with a huge sob. Esi put his arm around the sobbing boy's shoulders and led him into the pantry.

The captain went to his side board and poured him and the cox a glass of port.

"That is an impressive mind we have there, John. I am continually amazed at his resilience and clarity of thought. Who would have thought that he would grasp the concept of the four percent's after just one meeting with the bank?"

"Aye. I listened in as you asked, and he was right on it as soon as old Spinner told him about it," John replied. At the captain's request, he had discretely cast a watchful eye over Marty on his visit into town. They had worried that he would get carried away with his new-found wealth, so John had preceded him into the bank and listened in on the meeting.

"Hmm. My sister thinks of him as the son she never had and the Count talks of him like a nephew. With 'family' like that, he can't go far wrong but where on earth did he get to be so ..... so .... smart from his background? I have met his family and none of them have his brains."

"Aye, sometimes he amazes me." John observed. "He has the heart of a lion and is already ahead of the other mids his age in navigation, he is the devil himself in a fight, and he has the respect of the men in his division." He paused as he listened to the sobbing coming from the Pantry. "I almost forget he be but a young lad away from 'ome fer the first time."

Marty met the captain by the entry port the next morning for their visit to the bank. His eyes were a little red, and he stood a little too erect with his shoulders a little too square. The captain asked if he was well and indicated he should precede him into the barge. The trip across to the dock was uneventful and they made quick time to the bank.

"Young Mr. Stockley here has a need to help his family after a recent misfortune, Mr. Skinner, and we think you can help. Marty, please explain your idea."

"Well sir, I understood what you told me about the four percents yesterday and I want ter set something up fer to 'elp me family now me pop cain't werk. I had the idea that we could put a bunch of money into the fund and me family could be paid the interest to help them live comfortable like."

"How much per year would you like them to receive?" asked Mr. skinner.

"I reckon that a couple a quid a month plus the money from me pay should do 'em right."

Mr. Skinner made a quick calculation and said.

"Well I believe a trust fund of six hundred pounds should be enough to cover that. Now, how do we pay it to them?"

Marty looked at the captain. He hadn't thought about that!

"It should be transferred to my sister's account," he said, "she will make sure the family get what they are due. She knows Mr. Stockley's mother quite well."

Marty nodded and waited to see what happened next.

"I will prepare the papers to set up the fund and to pay the interest to your sister, Captain Turner. We have her details already, I believe. They will be ready for signature tomorrow afternoon, and we will send copies to our London office on the next packet so the fund can be established as soon as possible."

"How long will it be before they gets any money?" asked Marty.

"Well, they will see the first income from the fund after one year," replied Skinner.

Marty paused for thought and then asked the captain,

"Kin I send Miss Turner twenty-four quid to give me mam two quid a month till the fund starts payin'?"

"Well, of course you can," he said, "Is there anything else you want to do?"

"Yes," said Marty, "I want to buy me mam an 'ouse where she can be comfortable and look after pop and grandpa. When me brothers and sisters is all married and left, then the mine won't let them live in their 'ouse anymore."

"Excellent investment," said Skinner, prompting Marty to give him a narrow-eyed look.

"I will instruct the bank to have an agent look for a suitable property."

"That won't be necessary," said Captain Turner. He winked and smiled at Marty. "My sister is very familiar with the area and can find a suitable property. It will keep her busy. We will write to her directly."

"As you wish," said Skinner who obviously didn't think that was a good idea at all.

Back onboard the Falcon, Marty sat down and wrote new letters to his mother and Miss Turner. He explained to both of them what he was doing and if there were any doctors bills for his father that they should be passed to him and he would make sure they were paid in full. He also asked Miss Turner to make sure the house for his mother was big enough for her to have a room of her own where she could relax when not caring for his father and grandfather.

The next morning, Cox John, as he was beginning to know him, accompanied him to the bank to sign the papers with Captain Turner being too busy. It was an uneventful trip and he felt the need to distract himself from thinking about his family and especially the loss of his brother.

So, once he finished his watch, he threw himself into weapons practice. Lieutenant Dicky was up and about, recuperating well and looking for exercise as well, so the two paired off and started fencing. Dicky was an accomplished fencer and made up for his lame leg with a wickedly fast wrist and a longer reach. Marty was still learning, but his grief gave him energy and he held his own. Their contest started to draw a crowd as off-watch sailors, and some of their fellow officers gathered to watch the display. Attracted by the noise of clashing blades the captain came to the rail at the front of the quarterdeck, where he had been taking the air, to see what was going on.

It was a warm day at the start of the Mediterranean spring. Dicky's guard was superb, and Marty probed and tested it with as many combinations as he could think of. He had to be careful as well as he knew that Dicky was a clever counter puncher and if he made a mistake and over extended, he would pay for it. Both of them were sweating and Marty's wrist was beginning to ache, but he could also see that Dicky was becoming more sedentary as the exercise took its toll on his wounded leg.

In the end, the captain called,

"Hold! I believe we have witnessed a draw and an excellent display of swordsmanship. Mr. Dicky, I believe you should rest that leg of yours now."

The two stood back equally convinced they would have won. Dicky grinned at Marty and raised his sword in salute. Marty, coming out of the zone he had worked himself into, grinned back, and saluted as well.

While Dicky returned to his quarters to rest, Marty still felt the need to do something, so he went and got his pistols, found a quiet spot on deck in the sunshine, and proceeded to strip them down for a good clean. He removed the barrels, carefully unloaded them, then removed the action. He carefully and meticulously cleaned each part, checked for wear and carefully oiled each component. He reassembled each gun and reloaded them.

"You think you are a fair shot?" the voice of Lieutenant La Pierre of the Marines said in his ear. Marty jumped as he had been engrossed in his efforts and hadn't heard him walk up behind him.

"Would you like to try yourself against me?" La Pierre asked him. Marty went to pick up his pistols, but La Pierre shook his head and held out two beautiful duelling pistols. "They were made by Nock like your pepper pots," he explained as he handed one to Marty, "and are perfectly matched." Marty examined the pistol, which had an octagonal, nine and a half inch, seventy five calibre barrel, and a beautifully engraved action. There were rear and foresights fitted, and the trigger guards were inlaid with silver.

They moved down to the fore deck and La Pierre had one of his men string some bottles up from the foremast lower yard. They stood side by side some forty feet from their targets and La Pierre showed Marty how to stand side on "to present your opponent with a smaller target" and raise the already cocked gun up at arm's length, aim, and fire. His first shot smashed the bottle.

Marty's turn. He raised the gun as he was shown. It was quite heavy but not unmanageable and to his surprise, it went off before he had properly aimed it. La Pierre chuckled at the look of surprise on Marty's face. "Hair trigger," he said, "keep your finger away from it until you are ready to fire." They reloaded. This time, Marty kept his index finger laying alongside the trigger until he had the target in his sights. He then gently slid his finger through the guard, took a deep breath, held it, and squeezed. The hammer came forward and the flint struck the frizzen, creating a shower of sparks that, as the frizzen plate swung forward exposing the priming pan, ignited the priming powder. There was a whoosh and then a bang as the main charge exploded in the barrel sending the ball on its way. He missed but not by much.

"Not bad for your first try," said La Pierre, "try again," and handed him the second pistol. Marty went through the routine again. Cock, Raise, Aim, Squeeze. This time, he hit his target and the bottle smashed! "Good," praised La Pierre, "let's see if you can do that again." They stayed there for an hour taking turns at shooting bottles until Marty's arm started to shake as he raised it, at which point La Pierre called a halt. Midshipman Clegg approached them and said, "Captain's complements gentlemen, and he would be obliged if you clean up all that glass from his deck before you finish."

"Got it covered, old chap," laughed La Pierre and signalled to the Marines who had been setting up the targets. Brooms appeared, and the scattered remains were soon swept in to a pile and dumped overboard. The lieutenant took Marty by the arm and led him to the wardroom. Once there, he poured him a glass of Rhenish wine that was dry, fruity, and cool having been stored in the bilge. They talked, and Marty learned that La Pierre was twenty-four years old and his family were land owners in Kent. He was the youngest of three sons and had chosen the Marines as a profession rather than the clergy, which his mother had wanted him to go into. Despite the almost seven-year gap in their ages, Marty felt that he had made a friend with the suave and elegant young man who was quite the rake in his own right.

Lieutenant Gentry came in and Marty jumped to his feet only to be waved back to his chair. "I've been given command of the Forfait!" he announced as Lieutenant Dicky stuck his head out of his cabin. Congratulations were given by all of them, but there was no time for celebration as 'Captain Gentry' was to report to his new command immediately. Marty was waiting for Graveny to be made first but is wasn't to be, a boat approached from the Flagship.

Vice Admiral Lord Hotham was running things for Hood in his absence and was making his interests known. He had promoted his second, Steven Hill, to be first in Falcon. Hill made quite an impression when he came onboard. He was not overly tall at around five foot eight, had bright red hair, wore a very well-made uniform with what looked like, a new bicorn hat worn across thwarts. The three very large pieces of luggage that followed him up were impressive as well, causing Dicky to snigger.

"Don't think he's lived on a Frigate before." as they alone would fill his first lieutenant's cabin.

The captain obviously noticed as well, as after he had reported to him, Hill was seen rapidly rearranging the contents and then sending two of the three down into the hold. What was welcome with the incumbent lieutenants was the number of personal stores he brought with him. The comment "we won't go short this trip" was overheard more than once.

He made himself known almost immediately his belongings were stowed. He called the lieutenants together in the wardroom along with La Pierre of the Marines, introduced himself and gave them a short talk on how he expected the ship to run. He also made it clear that the discipline and care of the mids was the responsibility of the Fourth and he didn't want anything to do with them outside of their duties. He said something about the hierarchy of command or some such.

The rumour eventually filtered down to Marty that Hill was the 'nephew' of the admiral's mistress and had joined the Navy directly as a lieutenant four years before. He had made second on the Flagship as a direct result of the admiral's interest. Now, he had been given this chance to get some real sea experience, probably for the first time, in the Falcon.

From his duties as assistant clerk, he discovered that the Forfait, now called the Fortune, had been bought in and classified as a Sloop of War. She was being fitted out with sixteen six-pounders and four carronades to replace the French guns that she had come with.

She had one hundred and fifty men on board mainly from the sloop Amalie, which had her bottom ripped out when she ran aground trying to cut the corner into the harbour. Her disgraced and highly embarrassed former Master and Commander, Lieutenant Francis Arkwright, was waiting for Courts Marshal.

He also knew that the Fortune was to accompany them on patrol. Both the Fortune and the Falcon were being repaired by the yard and were forecast to be finished within a day of each other. On the advice of Tom, Marty made sure he did his work diligently and stayed out of the new First's way.

Another addition was a new mid. Cecil Braithwaite, who was nine years old and had never left home, let alone been at sea before. He was brought on board by his father the day they completed their repairs with his mother crying on the dock, and waving a handkerchief in farewell, as they were rowed across. It transpired that his father was the carpenter in chief in the docks and part of his demands to get the two ships repaired had been that the captain took his youngest son on as a midshipman.

They were preparing to set out to sea when, Marty, who was in charge of the boys that were nipping the messenger line to the anchor hawse, looked across at the Fortune just as a shape fell from the main topsail yard. A second after he saw it, he heard the scream, shrill and young. It seemed to go on forever until it stopped abruptly as the body hit the deck rail and bounced over the side.

"MAN O'RBOARD THE FORTUNE," Marty yelled at the top of his voice. He looked around at the quarterdeck where the new first lieutenant stood at the rail with his eyes wide and his mouth open. The captain, however, wasn't shocked to a standstill. "AVAST HAULIN'," he called and the men at the capstan stopped pushing at the bars. "Mr. Dicky, get over there and see what the hell is going on!"

Richard called out orders and the gig was hauled around from astern, a crew assembled, and he was on his way in a matter of minutes. It didn't take much longer for him to return along with Captain Gentry. Both of them went directly to the quarterdeck. During the following conversation, Gentry turned and waved a hand at Marty before turning back to talk to Captain Turner. The captain looked a little put out but nodded. He looked over at Marty, pointed at him, and beckoned him up to the quarterdeck.

"Mr. Stockley, it would appear Captain Gentry has need of your services on the Fortune, for a time," he seemed to emphasize the last three words and looked at Gentry, who smiled when he said it. "So, be so kind as to get your sea chest and be ready to accompany him back to the Fortune. I am sure the good commander will wait for you."

He looked over at Lieutenant Hill disapproval writ clear on his face, "Mr. Hill, if you would be so kind to attend me in my cabin."

He nodded politely to Gentry and Martin and left the quarterdeck with a final "Mr. Rampole, you have the deck. Please take us out as soon as Commander Gentry and Midshipman Stockley are aboard the Fortune."

Marty made short work of picking up his chest and was back up on deck at the entry port in short order. His chest was passed down and he preceded Gentry into the gig. Just as he sat, he noticed that the oars were manned by Tom Savage, John Smith the fifth' and the four Basques. As Commander Gentry joined him, he nodded to the men. "I got you as long as I took these sorry excuses for seamen along in exchange for six, I am sending back with the gig. Seems you lot come as a package, but I'll not look a gift horse in the mouth."

Once back aboard, six men were called, after they had retrieved their sea bags, boarded the gig and pulled over to the Falcon as she was starting to weigh anchor again.

Once they were at sea, Commander Gentry asked Marty to attend him in his quarters. He was announced by a marine and entered. "Mr. Stockley, welcome. Please be seated," said Commander Gentry. "I gather you saw the incident in the harbour?" he asked

"Aye, sir, I saw someone fall and raised the alarm," Marty replied.

"Yes, well Fletcher was my second mid. He broke his back on the rail and didn't survive the dunking in the harbour." He stood and looked out of the stern windows. "He was recommended to me by the port admiral and was experienced. He was to help bring the crew from the Amalie into line. They are an ill-disciplined lot. Their Commander treated his command as some kind of pleasure cruise and the ship as his private yacht." He paused as if considering how much to say and then with a sigh continued. "I am not sure if he fell, or he was pushed. I need help to instil discipline and to make this an efficient ship, which is why I asked for you. You seem to have the knack of getting the best out of men and, with your happy band of followers, you can set an example and maybe provide some leadership. You can also ask them to keep their ears to the mast and see if they can find out anything about what happened to young Fletcher."

Leadership? thought Marty in surprise. He had never in his life thought of himself as a leader.

"I'll do my best, sir," he said out loud, privately wondering what the hell had Commander Gentry gotten him into.

Chapter 12: Patrol

Marty could feel that the ship wasn't happy. Most of the sailors went about their business grudgingly not liking to be pushed at Navy speed or the discipline. It became obvious to Marty that Arkwright had only been interested in sailing and had spoiled the sail handlers and haulers to the detriment of his gun crews and the other sailors.

He had the chance to watch them and soon picked out the worst offenders. One was a seaman who, if what he heard was true, had signed up with the previous commander because he was promised a leisure cruise and resented being dragged into the Navy proper. The man, Wilson, was big and was chosen for his strength at hauling up sails rather than anything else. Apparently, he and the rest of the 'Gorillas' had been treated preferentially by Commander Arkwright, given better food and extra drink rations. Another was a foretopman and a third was the captain of the maintop. He thought that if those men weren't agitating, the crew would probably settle.

He reported his observations and intelligence to Commander Gentry, who had suspected the same and said he would think about how to proceed. In the meantime, Gentry had a made up a new watchlist and had put Wilson in one of Marty's gun crews. Gun practice started as soon as they were in the Mediterranean proper and it was criminal how bad they were.

On a ship this size, with only two lieutenants and three midshipmen, Marty had the after four six pounders and the two carronades on the after deck, which was just an extension of the main deck. The oldest mid, Andrew Sheldon, had the forward four six pounders and the youngest Arnold Rachford was designated signals. The First Lieutenant oversaw all activities and the Second focused his attention on activities forward of the main mast. They should never need to fire both broadsides at the same time on a Sloop so the gun crews would change sides as required.

Marty set about trying to improve the performance of his gun crews. His Basques were distributed amongst the topmen, so he only had Tom Savage and John Smith from the Falcon. He figured repetition was part of the cure, so he had them run the guns in, load, and run out in a dumb show of firing, drilling the men on the routine steps. He moved from gun to gun making sure the men were in the right positions to avoid getting hurt. He wasn't at all surprised to find that Wilson resented being told what to do by a mere child as he saw it.

Later that day as the men had their evening meal, Marty was just about to pass through the deck where the men lived and ate when he heard Wilson telling anybody that could hear that he would put Marty over his knee and give him a thrashing if he didn't stop pushing him around. Marty was about to step forward and confront him when the quieter and amused voice of John Smith said,

"You reckon you could, do you?"

Wilson scoffed and replied.

"What is he thirteen or fourteen-year-old? He ain't big enough to get my respect and he ain't too big for a thrashing."

"How many men you killed Wilson?" asked John.

There was a silence and then Wilson said.

"That bain't be the point. He is a kid and he can go the same way as that other snot."

"Really? You claiming to 'ave done fer that younger?" said John, leaning closer.

Wilson leaned back away from him and said,

"I ain't claimin' nuffin, just sayin is all."

So repeated John. "You ain't killed a man at least not face ter face,"

"What you getting' at?" snarled Wilson, "you accusing me of somit?

"Not at all," said John, "but you got ter know that, there 'boy' saved Captain Taylor of the Falcon's life when he were just a cabin boy. Killed a Frenchy with his knife, you aint seen that yet it's a big nasty bugger, by shoving it through his heart, another by cutting his bollocks off wiv a tomahawk. He have took out a couple or three with his pistols, which you also ain't seen yet, and he done fer the skipper of this here ship when we captured it when he attacked 'im from behind. He thought he were only taking on a boy too." He had his audience's attention now, and they prompted him for the tale of the rescue of the count. He was just getting in to it when Marty decided enough was enough.

"That'll do, John," he said, stepping into the light. The men were startled at his sudden appearance and the flickering lanthorn light made him look somewhat eerie.

"Tomorrow this division will have weapons practice." He told them. "Let's see how you gentlemen fair with a blade in your hands." He looked directly at Wilson as he said it. "Get a good night's sleep. You will need all your energy tomorrow." He turned to leave and caught John's eye which he dropped in a very slight wink.

The next morning after the regular work for his division was completed, the men gathered between the main and fore masts. He went below and changed into his fighting uniform which still showed extensive blood stains and repair, and he wore his weapons belts with his hanger, knife, and pistols all in place. When he got up on deck his Basques were waiting along the rail to watch, as he had asked, and when they saw him gave their most evil grins.

He called his men to get their attention. The looks on all the ex-Amalie's faces as they took in the blood-stained uniform showed he was making an impression. They ranged from wide eyed horror at the evidence of terminal violence to thoughtful contemplation. Tom and John stood off to one side and looked to be thoroughly enjoying themselves. Marty took out his pistols and handed them to Pablo, warning him they were loaded. At the look of surprise on the face of the nearest man he said, "an empty gun be nothin' but a club."

He pulled out his hanger and pointed it at the man next to Wilson, who he figured was one of his cronies.

"You! Get a cutlass and step over here," he said, indicating the clear area of deck. As the man stepped up, Marty took a casual, low guard with his sword to the front, point low.

"What's yer name?"

"Simms," he replied.

Marty looked him in the eye.

"Simms what?" he looked confused and then someone prompted him with a hissed whisper, and he stuttered,

"Simms, Sir."

"Attack me." Marty said. Simms looked confused again and didn't move so Marty said it again.

"Don't just stand there with your prick in your hand. ATTACK ME." Simms looked down at his sword and held it out in front of him a bit like he was holding a flower, so Marty stepped forward, slapped it close to the hilt, making him drop it and then jabbed him over the heart with his sword.

"You are dead. Get back into line. You either attack and beat the other man or you die. Next!"

This time, Wilson stepped forward and took the cutlass from Simms. He muttered something then came forward and swung it a couple of times like it was a sickle or an axe. Marty grinned and reached behind him for his fighting knife and as it came into view, there was an audible gasp from the men. The blade looked huge in his hand and glinted wickedly in the sunlight.

Wilson immediately said, "That ain't fair you got two blades."

Marty looked over to Tom and said, "you tell 'im."

Tom grinned and said, "Well it be like this, mate. Them Frenchy's don't give a rat's cock for whether a fight be fair or not. They be just out to kill 'e so if'n I was you I'd make sure I never gives 'em the chance."

Wilson snarled something illegible in reply and stepped forward, swinging like he was trying to cut Marty in half at the waist. Marty had expected that, and he swayed back away from the blade and let it go by. As Wilson was carried by the momentum, he stepped behind him and slapped him on the thigh with the flat of his hanger.

"Dead," he said. "Try again." Wilson was enraged and took up his stance again. This time, he tried an overhead slash and was totally surprised when Marty stepped forward and raised his hanger at an angle in high parry so that the cutlass slid off to the side. His left hand came around and the point of his fighting knife was tickling Wilson's ribs just hard enough to draw a little blood.

"You're dead again," he said softly. "Want to play some more?" Wilson, eyes wide, shook his head.

Marty stepped back. "You will all learn the basics of close quarters fighting. We will also practice boxing and street fighting. I don't want any of my men killed through not knowin' 'ow to fight," he said. He could see Wilson was being joshed by his mates.

"You don't have to be big to win a fight," he continued, "you just need to know a bit more than the other man. These men," he indicated the four Basques plus Tom savage and John Smith, "will be your instructors. I will teach the rudiments of knife fighting. If you think you are already a half decent knife fighter, come to me now. Otherwise, pair off with your weapons of choice."

The session went fairly well after that. There were a couple of men who fancied themselves as knife fighters and found out early on that they weren't anywhere near as good as they thought. Marty showed them some of the standard moves and had them practice on each other.

The Basque Boys had a direct, brutal, and effective way of teaching close in deck fighting with knife, tomahawk, or marlin spike. Men were paired up and the moves demonstrated to grunts of pain from the victims. Tom and John had great fun showing the men how to swing a cutlass without cutting their own or their neighbour's ears off. Nobody got seriously cut and nobody died. Even Wilson seemed to put his back into it after a while.

At the end of the session, Marty was asked to demonstrate his pistols, which he did by emulating La Pierre and hanging a few bottles by cords from the foremast main yard and shooting them from ten paces. He then invited two men who had admitted having at least shot something before to try. One surprised him and nicked his bottle while the other missed by a mile.

All in all, it wasn't too bad for the first session. There were numerous bruises but more of a team feeling than he had before. He had it in mind to suggest inter-division competitions to the captain.

After a week of dumb show on the cannons, the captain ordered the first live fire exercise. First, without ball loaded and then with. Marty's men were in position and the cartridge was brought up from the magazine by the ship's boys.

The order was given, and the guns were pulled back and loaded with just a wad packed down on top of the powder. The gun was pulled up to the port and the gun captain made a mime of aiming it. The men stood away and the line from the flintlock igniter was stretched out behind the gun so the gun captain would be clear of the recoil when he triggered it. BOOM, the first gun fired followed by all nine in sequence except the number eight which had a misfire. Before Marty could stop him, Wilson stepped up to the gun to look at the flintlock and that is exactly when the charge ignited, and the recoil sent the carriage back over the toes of his left foot.

Marty yelled for the surgeon and ran to make sure the man was in no further danger. He had him dragged away from the gun to the centreline of the ship and once he was being attended to, he turned back to the gun and took his place. He continued shouting instructions and working with the men until the exercise was over.

He visited the surgeon on the Orlop deck as soon as he was free and asked after Wilson. Laithwaite, the surgeon, told him that Wilson had been lucky; his foot had been at an angle and only three toes had been crushed. His big toe and the one next to it would be OK. He had already removed the crushed toes and cauterized the wounds. "If he stays off it for a couple of weeks, he should make a full recovery," was the prognosis.

Marty went to report to the captain and when he entered his quarters, he was asked to sit down.

"What have you to report, Mr. Stockley?" he was asked

"I've 'eard nothing more about the fall of Midshipman Fletcher other than one of the topmen said 'e was trying to tell all of them 'ow to do their jobs when 'e missed his footing and fell. Nobody else 'as said anything to support that.

With the guns, we managed two rounds in just under three minutes," he said. "Which isn't bad considering that a week ago they were taking two minutes to fire one. I wouldn't want to get into a pounding match with a Frenchie of the same size yet, but they are improving."

"Hmm, it's the same on the other guns. We need to keep up the practice. I don't think Arkright ever exercised the guns in the two years he had command. Now, how is your wounded man? He was one of the troublemakers, wasn't he?"

Marty reported what the surgeon had told him and commented, "He has been less aggressive since we started weapons and gun training although he still reckons that I could do with a spanking."

Gentry laughed at that and said, "I would like to see him try! You would probably gut him with your Midshipman's dirk. Now, I saw you manning his place on the gun and that cannot continue so I will assign a new man to you. He is a landsman and you will have to whip him into shape."

"Thankee, sir," said Marty.

"Midshipman Rachford Saah!" bellowed the Marine sentry.

"Enter," said the Captain.

"Mr. Forde's compliments," he said, "But the Falcon has signalled 'Enemy in sight'."

The captain replied, "Give Mr. Forde my thanks and tell him I will be on deck directly." To Marty he said, "you had better get back to your division, we may be heading into a fight."

Marty followed the captain on deck and heard the report that there had been a couple of ships sighted to the Northwest. The Frigates mast being that much taller had enabled their lookouts to see them earlier but now the target ships were visible to their lookouts.

"Two ships to the Northwest!" Cried the main mast lookout

"Look like they are heading East across our course!"

Then after a pause of several minutes, "Deck there! Looks like one is a Polacre and the other a Snow."

"Falcon is signalling, sir. Our number and pursue."

"Make all sail and let's get up with the Falcon. I want us to pass half a cable off her Starboard beam." Said the Captain.

With the extra sail on the smaller ship came up on the Frigate and they heard the clarion call of the hunting horn. Captain Turner pointed at their prey and gestured for them to go ahead as they were faster. Gentry had them come two points to Starboard. Now, the superior sail handling qualities of the crew came into their own as the Fortune fairly leapt away and the chase was on.

Marty went below, changed into his fighting uniform and donned his weapons. He checked his blades for sharpness and decided they could do with a lick of the grindstone.

On deck, he went to the armorer who had the big sharpening wheel up and was applying an edge to a pile of cutlasses. Marty tapped him on the shoulder, handed him his knife and hanger, then went to check on his guns. The first had called for the ship to be cleared for action and his men were in their places. Some looked excited, some scared, and some as if this happened every day. To his utter surprise, there was Wilson at his gun, his foot wrapped in what looked like an old shirt that was bound in leather strips to hold it in place. If Marty had ever seen one, he would have thought it looked a bit like a Roman sandal.

When confronted, Wilson said, "I aint missing our first fight! And you need me cus I know the drill and that other bugger don't!"

The 'other bugger' was standing to the side looking somewhat bemused and at a loss as what to do.

"You!" Marty barked.

"What's your name?"

"Bevan, sir," he replied with a decided Welsh accent.

"You are our reserve. If anyone drops off a gun, take his place. Do exactly what you are told. Understood?"

"Aye Aye, sir," he said, touching his forelock.

Lord, help us if we do, Marty thought as he went back to the armourer to retrieve his now razor-sharp weapons.

The captain's plan unfolded. They were taking a course to cut the targets off from sailing East. Then the lookout called down that he could see that they were definitely French, and that they were now steering more to the North.

A stern chase is a long chase, he thought but kept it to himself.

An hour or so later saw them closing steadily on their prey. A look over his shoulder to Larboard showed the Falcon had shaken out her skirts and had everything including studding sails set but was still falling behind. Marty looked up to see that Rachford stood near him. The young lieutenant grinned at him and said,

"Sails like a witch, don't she?"

"Aye, that she does," answered Marty and grinned back.

Looking forward, they could see that they were slowly gaining, and the First Lieutenant and the master were both using their sextants to take the angle to the Frenchies masts so they could work out the range.

It was still another hour until the command came for the fore chasers to be readied. These were brass long nines that had been found in the gun yard in Gibraltar. They were well made, had true bores, and could throw a nine-pound ball a good mile or more with some accuracy. Some serious bribes had changed hands to obtain them as they technically put the Fortune over her compliment of long guns, but Gentry had fallen in love with them and thought the cost was worth it.

He watched as the Gunner himself laid the Starboard gun, then stepped back and pulled the lanyard just as the bow was reaching the peak of the up roll. From directly behind, he could see the ball as it shot out of the cloud of smoke in direct line with the Snow and saw it plunge into the sea just short of their stern. He returned his gaze to the foredeck and now the gunner was on the larboard gun and pulling the lanyard. He followed the ball again and this time, he saw it hit the snow on the transom, their colours came tumbling down as she turned into wind.

"She's struck!" went up the shout and the crew started cheering.

"AVAST THAT, QUIET ON MY SHIP" roared the voice of the First Lieutenant.

They were evidently not going to stop for their prize and were leaving it to the Falcon to secure it as they continued the pursuit of the Polacre. The Frenchman tried coming up harder in to the wind in an attempt to gain a fraction more speed. But that gave them an angle they could use to bear down on him all the faster, and soon they were ready to try the long nines again. They fired first one then the other but no hits. They reloaded and were about to try again when the Frenchman swerved to Starboard and loosed of his four six pounders in broadside. He missed and all his efforts got him was the Fortune sliding up even closer.

The captain called, "Ready the Larboard guns. Double shotted!" Marty ran from gun to gun, making sure they were loaded correctly. This wasn't something they had practiced yet.

"READY! On the up-roll. FIRE!"

The Fortune swung to Starboard, and her guns came into line with the Frenchman. Marty was behind the number nine gun looking down the barrel. He watched as the horizon dropped and then slowed. "FIRE," yelled Lieutenant Forde and all nine guns spoke almost in unison. The Fortune swung back on course as the men swabbed out the barrels and reloaded. Marty looked toward the Frenchman, but he couldn't see any damage and she was still sailing as hard as ever. The Fore chasers barked again but he couldn't stand and watch this time as he was calling out the steps to his men. A cheer!

There must have been at least one hit, he thought.

They were ready. A glance over the side showed the French ship much closer. Their superior sail handling was still telling. Another swing to Starboard.

"ON THE UPROLL! FIRE!" The guns spoke again. This time, there was an answering bark from the other ship and shot whistled through the rigging. Men looked up and Marty shouted at them to concentrate and marked the steps to reload. The noise and smoke confused some and Marty was frantically going from gun to gun pushing and shoving men into position and shouting the next steps to them. He looked up; the Frenchman was less than a musket shot away. Again, the order "FIRE," and when the smoke cleared, he saw star shaped holes in her side and some rigging flapping.

"CARRONADES," called the first lieutenant. Marty stepped over to them. They were preloaded with grape, and he aimed them at the other ships quarterdeck. He had the shot, so he didn't wait. He yelled, "FIRE," and they both chuffed their deadly load together. This time, he was watching and through the smoke he saw the grape shot rip across the deck shredding anything in its way.

This was too much for the French and a sailor ran to the stern and cut down the colours as she let the wind out of her sails in surrender.

Marty told his carronade crews to reload with canister in case the French changed their minds. Then he went down the line of the six pounders checking on each man and having a word with them to praise or to correct.

The second lieutenant, six marines, and ten sailors went across as a prize crew to take charge of the ship that was named La Fleur. Lieutenant Forde hailed across for the carpenter and ten more hands to help repair some of the damage so they could get her moving.

Le Fleur was an old ship but had been maintained well. She was a merchantman and was carrying corn and rice. She was armed with eight old six pounders. Forde reported the captain was dead, killed in the sweep of grape from the carronades, his master's mate was the most senior man on board and was the one who had struck. The crew numbered thirty, which seemed very few for a ship of that size.

Once they got back under sail they rendezvoused with the Falcon and the ther prize the "Joan." She had a mixed cargo of timber, nails, cheap wine, and various other general goods. Richard Dicky got command of her with a prize crew.

Captain Taylor called all the senior officers together for a conference. When Captain Gentry returned, they heard that they were to continue North to Toulon as a group. When they had made their initial survey, the Fortune would escort the prizes back to Gibraltar and deliver the report while the Falcon continued her patrol. The Fortune would return with the prize crews, and rendezvous with the Falcon at a pre-arranged latitude, which the Falcon would return to once a week from three weeks' hence.

The trip up the French coast was uneventful, partly because they were all flying French flags, a legitimate Ruse de Guerre as long as they showed their true colours before opened fire on anyone. The passed Perpignan, Montpellier, Marseille, and then Toulon. Each time, the Fortune would duck in close to the ports and see what ships were there. They also noted what shipping was moving along the coast. They didn't try and take more prizes as the information was more important. Once they reached Toulon, they looked in as far as they could and counted the warships in the harbour. One first rate, two Second, four fourths and seven of frigate size all with their yards crossed. With the information and Captain Turner's report secured on both the Fortune and the Snow, they turned South and headed for Gibraltar.

The captain had continued the training exercises during the trip North and didn't see why they should stop on the way back. Marty's division were steadily improving and he his skills as a gunner with them. They, even Wilson, grew to respect his natural talent as a fighter and the way he continuously honed that skill, like he did all the skills required of a prospective officer. The usual contrary winds made the journey longer and gave them more time to practice.

They came across a French Brig just off Barcelona, who obligingly sailed up to exchange news with what he thought was a French warship escorting two merchantmen. The captain had Pablo call across and invite the captain over for a glass of wine and an exchange of news. Once he was on board and out of sight, they grabbed him and stripped his clothes. Meanwhile, Pablo and the other Basques got his boat crew up on deck with the offer of some brandy and also snagged them.

They swapped clothes with the crewmen, and as the brig's Captain was only a small man, Marty was dressed in his clothes. The man's coat concealed his knife and guns. He made a show of waving goodbye as he clambered down into the small boat and kept his head down as his men rowed him over. He clambered up the side closely followed by the Basques. The master's mate got the fright of his life when he produced a gun and waved it under his nose. The rest of his men spread out and quickly rounded up the merchant crew and disposed of any weapons by throwing them over the side. As soon as he had control, he waved to the Fortune and a boat was sent over with another eight men.

Midshipman Sheldon came with them. Marty assumed that he was going to take over command of the Brig, but to his surprise he had Marty's sea chest and a packet from Captain Gentry.

"Captain's complements Martin, you are to take command of this ship with the men made available to you and sail her in convoy with us to Gibraltar. Here are your written orders." He broke out in a huge grin and held his hand out. As Marty shook it, he said, "He wanted me to take it, but you captured it, so I figured you should sail it in." He looked across at the extra eight men and said. "These all volunteered to come over. You have a master's mate, top men, and general hands. With only two masts to worry about, you should be fine." Marty looked around at the men and spotted Tom, John, and to his surprise, Wilson.

Twelve men plus him and all he had to do, if all went well, was follow the ship in front and try not to ram her up the stern. Should be a walk in the park.

Chapter 13: No Rest For The Wicked

The voyage back to Gibraltar was uneventful apart from the weather, which turned nasty as they turned towards the West around the corner of Spain, causing them to tack back and forth all the way from the Gulf of Almeria to the straits. He found that Wilson was a changed man. Instead of the grumpy, resentful person he had first met, he now willingly threw himself into the work and didn't complain any more than the rest of the men. When Marty asked Tom about it, he said,

"Once we started training on the guns and you started weapon drills, it were if he suddenly got what the Navy was really about." He thought for a second and then added with a chuckle. "The prize money didn't 'urt either." He pronounced either 'eever'. While Wilson would never be one of his "Shadow six," he nevertheless was turning in to a loyal part of Marty's team and that was a good thing in his mind.

When they eventually got into port, Gentry reported immediately to the admiral and the prize crews were replaced by men from the port admiral's staff who started inventorying everything. Prisoners were shipped ashore, and the Falcons and Fortunes made their way back to the Fortune.

The first immediately took on stores, not just for them but to replenish the Falcon when they rendezvoused. Everybody who could grabbed the chance to get in some personal stores.

Nothing was said about him commanding the prize but by all accounts, the admiral was very happy with the haul (probably looking forward to his share) and the intelligence report disappeared into his desk without comment. As they had only been away for just over a month, there was no mail, but they could live with that. In all, they were in port for just twenty-four hours when they started preparing to leave again.

Just before they left, a boat approached from the dock with an officer and a civilian in the stern. The officer was a flag lieutenant and carried a message pouch. The civilian had a bag with him and was dressed in a dark coat and a pepper pot hat like the French wore. The crew and the junior officers were intrigued.

The two of them went down into the captain's quarters and twenty minutes later, only the flag lieutenant came out. Intriguing.

They set sail and were well out to sea running before a fresh breeze before the man in the dark coat and hat was seen again. He came up from below and stood on the leeward side of the quarterdeck showing he at least knew something of Navy protocol. Marty didn't take a command watch on the Fortune as they ran a three-watch system and the two lieutenants and the senior mid took care of them. His responsibilities were solely with his division and his guns, so he didn't get a chance to talk to the stranger until after they had been at sea for around four days. He was sitting practicing his knots, deep in concentration when a soft voice with a decidedly French accent said,

"Do I 'av ze pleasure of addressing Messieurs Stockley?"

Marty nearly jumped out of his skin and his hand was halfway to his dirk before he realized it was the Stanger.

"Oui, Messieurs," he said, remembering the lessons Evelyn had given him.

"I would like to zank you for rescuing mon amie le Conte de Marchets, it is certainement that zey would av perished if zey 'ad stayed in Toulon," he said and held out his hand.

Marty stood and took it, and said.

"It were the least I could do. He is a proper gentleman and a friend to me."

"Oui, he told me about you and said that if ever I needed help to ask for you as you were very capable."

Oh Christ, where is this going, thought Marty.

"I av talked wiz your Capitain and he as reluctantly agreed to mon request." Marty raised his eyebrows.

"I av to admit I 'ad to use mon connexion to your Admiral 'ood and ze authority 'e 'az given me, mon mission az to take ze priority."

He looked around and saw that several men were watching him closely. Marty noticed that they were mainly men from his division.

"Let uz go zomewhere more private," he said, took Marty by the arm and led him to the captain's cabin. To his surprise, the Marine just opened the door and let them in unannounced.

Once inside, they were alone as Gentry was taking a watch.

"I want you to accompany me on a mission into France," the stranger said in remarkably better English than he had spoken outside. Marty's eyes nearly popped out of his head in astonishment.

"I don't even know your name and you want me to go in to bloody France with you?" He squeaked, his voice betraying him.

The stranger looked at him steadily for a moment and then said, "You can call me Serge. What I am about to tell you can never be repeated. Do you understand?"

Marty got himself together and nodded as he didn't trust his own voice, nor did he trust that was his real name.

"We 'ave to go on shore into France near Marseille and make contact with some people who are no friends of the Republique. They 'av information that is vital to the British about the intentions of the French fleet in Toulon and ze destination when they sail," he explained.

"Our contact 'as to be very careful as he is in a position of trust in the ministry of marine and will only give the information to me as he knows me from a long time ago."

"So, why do yer need me?" asked Marty.

"The republic's secret police will be looking for a single man and will not notice a man with his son. Especially one that is a deaf mute."

"So, I won't 'ave to speak French then?" Marty asked.

"Non. Your accent is abominable, and you would never pass as a French boy," Serge replied.

"Can I take my weapons?"

"As long as they can be concealed. So, not your sword but that big knife of yours may be very 'andy."

Me knife and guns then, thought Marty, *and I reckon another knife in me boot won't go amiss.*

"We will be put ashore on a beach at a place called Callelongue. It is about a ten kilometre walk from there to the Abbaye Sain't Victor, where 'e will pass the information," added Serge.

They heard a stamp as the sentry came to attention then the door opened as Captain Gentry entered. He looked from one to the other and said,

"I saw you two talking on deck," he took off his coat and threw it over the back of a chair. "Have you agreed to go, Martin?"

First names, Marty thought, *why do they always use first names when they're getting you in the shit?*

But he answered, "Aye, Aye, sir. I be in."

Back in the cockpit, Marty had to avoid the questions from the other mids, who had seen him go below with Serge. Forde and Fleming, the lieutenants, must have been told something by the captain as they had just looked at him with worried frowns when they saw him later on deck.

Another day saw them passing Marseille. Callelongue was hidden behind the Isle Marie below the point at the South end of Marseilles Bay. To get ashore, they would heave to at dusk, South of the island as if they were just sheltering for the night, and then a boat would row them into the inlet and drop them off. The plan was that they would be picked up two days later an hour either side of dusk. If they weren't there, the Fortune would return the next two nights at the same time.

Marty was dressed as a farm boy with loose white shirt, waistcoat, and trousers with scruffy old boots. Serge as a farmer with a similar outfit. He couldn't hide his guns, so had to leave them behind and had to be happy just to have his fighting knife strapped to the small of his back with the hilt downwards. He secured it in its sheath with some fine thread that would stop the blade from sliding out under gravity but would break when he needed to pull the knife in anger. He concealed another knife that he got from Tom in a sheath strapped to his left forearm under his shirt. He added a third blade taken from a razor in the upper of his right boot concealed between the layers of leather by unstitching the top seam, sliding the blade in then replacing the stitching with a much lighter thread that could be unpicked with his fingers. This little addition would become a standard part of his dress from that time onwards.

They would circle around the town and approach from the landward side as if they had come in from the countryside.

The crew was intrigued to see their Marty dressed so strangely leaving the ship with a Frenchman. The boat crew, which Tom, John, Pablo and Matai had managed to get a seat on, were concerned and there was a lot of whispering going on. The boat entered the inlet and made its way inland for a hundred yards or so where they found an easy place to set them ashore. From there, they set off across the scrubby dunes in a generally North-westerly direction.

After about two hours of hard going, they struck a rough road heading into the town. Serge had them settle down near the road in the shelter of a hedge to rest until dawn. Marty was grateful for the break as the old boots had worn blisters on both his heels and one on the big toe of his right foot. He treated them by cutting them open and dousing neat brandy, from a small flask he had in his shoulder bag, into the cuts. It hurt like hell but hardened the skin up overnight.

The sun came up too soon in his mind, and Serge had them on the road as soon as it was light enough to see. The road was quiet at first, but soon there were carts and farmers driving everything from geese to steers into the town.

Now Marty understood Serge's timing. Another pair of farmers entering town at that time of day shouldn't be noticed at all. There were guards at a checkpoint, but they were more interested in stopping people with goods. Marty saw money change hands as bribes were paid. He kept his head down but eyes open, so he saw the man dressed in grey with non-descript features standing by the gate watching everyone who passed through.

Suddenly, Serge was confronted by a man in uniform with a cockade in his hat. The man made a demand and Serge produced a paper, which he handed over. The man looked at Marty and asked him something. Marty forced himself to look at him blankly. The man prodded him in the chest and Marty had no problem looking frightened and a bit confused. Serge grabbed Marty and pulled him under the lee of his arm, all the time talking earnestly to the man. To Marty's relief, the man thrust the paper back into Serge's hand and sent them on their way. Serge kept him close and led him along the road into the town.

They stopped in a marketplace and Serge got them a long, stick like bread. He broke a chunk off and handed to Marty along with a soft creamy cheese that smelt vaguely like cabbage but tasted lovely. They drank water from a fountain then continued their walk towards the Abbaye. Marty had a feeling they were being followed and tried to sneak a look back the way they had come, but he didn't spot anyone that stood out. He tried again a little later and this time saw a man in the same uniform as the one who confronted Serge. He had his hat pulled low over his face so he couldn't see what he looked like, but now that he had spotted him, he saw that the man held a course that was almost in their wake and although he never looked directly at them, Marty was convinced he was following them.

Nothing else happened and they reached the Abbaye just before noon. There were a lot of pilgrims.

"Thought the revolution did away with the church?" Marty asked Serge when they were sure they couldn't be overheard.

"In the South that hasn't taken hold like in Paris." He replied. "The country people in this part of France are more superstitious and religious than in the cities."

They waited for more than an hour and then Serge stood, stretched, took Marty's arm, and led him towards the entrance to the Abbaye. He whispered in Marty's ear,

"Stagger and fall when I poke you in the ribs."

They had to climb some steps to the door and just before the top, Marty felt an elbow in the ribs and feigned a trip, falling to the floor across the top step. A man dressed in a sombre back coat and a tall hat with a wide brim sporting a cockade in the band reached down, helped him up and as he gripped his hand, he felt a piece of paper press into his palm. Marty made a show of rubbing his knee and shin, which allowed him to push the paper into his boot.

They continued into the Abbaye and knelt in a pew where they bowed their heads in mock prayer. Marty was led to an alcove where a queue of people were shuffling forward to touch a casket containing the desiccated remains of some bones. Serge took his hand and pressed it against the glass loudly, pleading with the saint to cure his son's affliction. That done, they quietly left and started back toward the town gate. As they passed an alley, the grey man from the gate stepped out with a gun in his hand which was pointed straight at Serge's chest.

"*Monsieur Clavelle, how nice to see you again,*" he said in French. "*I am surprised you thought you could avoid recognition with such a poor disguise.*"

Marty didn't understand what was being said, but he knew a shit situation when he saw one. The man continued,

"the boy is a nice touch. Did you buy him? Or are his parents also traitors?"

Serge kept his hands in plain sight and his eyes on their accoster, *"I don't think we have had the pleasure of meeting before Monsieur ...?"* he said,

"Pierre Marie." The man said with a minuscule bow, *"of the Department of Internal Security."*

While this exchange was going on, Marty had been playing the imbecile and was working his right hand towards the knife strapped to his forearm. He had just gotten his hand on it when the man in uniform, that had been following them, suddenly appeared behind the grey man.

The stranger made a move and Marie stiffened with a look of surprise on his face which was replaced with a very dead look. As he started to collapse, Serge stepped forward and caught him under one arm whilst the other man took the other, concealing his blood-stained knife by holding it along his forearm. They quickly carried him into the alley. "Keep watch," muttered Serge in passing. Trying to look casual, Marty scanned the area, but no one seemed to have taken any notice.

Serge and the man came out of the alley and Marty's mouth almost hit his chin, the man in the uniform was Antton!

"What the hell are you doing here?" he exploded and then realized to his horror that he had spoken English. He glanced around and saw a couple of people had heard. Serge said something quietly to Antton, who pulled himself up and strutting like a cockerel pushing the two of them ahead of him saying something loudly in French.

Serge said quietly to Marty, "He has just announced we are under arrest and that we are to accompany him to the police headquarters." The onlookers nodded wisely and jeered half-heartedly.

Antton pushed them regularly and even cuffed them around the heads if they staggered until they had left the area and were away from prying eyes. They ducked in to another alley, and Serge beckoned them to get their heads close together so they could talk.

"We 'ave to get out of the city but we cannot leave where we came in as someone else there might know me. We must go more around to the East and leave in that direction. We will stay wiz our disguise. Us two will go ahead and Antton will follow behind to ensure we are not followed."

Marty and Serge left first and followed back alleys and side streets heading generally North. Antton followed at a reasonable distance, sauntering along as if he owned the place. They got to the Rue St Pierre and turned East along it to leave the town. It was about four in the afternoon and there were a steady stream of carts and people leaving after their days business. They walked beside a farm cart whose driver was dressed a little like them, hoping to blend in. Suddenly they heard the pounding of hooves and a squadron of Chasseurs cantered up from behind them. Marty was struck by the gleam of their tack, white tight-fitting trousers, tight fitting blue jacket with complex ties on the front and the red fur trimmed jacket/cape that was worn just on the left arm and shoulder. The tall bearskin hat with its even taller black plume made them look even more imposing.

Marty all but held his breath as they passed. Serge looked around and said something to a man that rode up on an old horse. He caught the words 'assassin' and 'traitor' and his guts clenched. Serge thanked him and went and spoke to the carter. Whatever was said was greeted with a nod and Serge urged him up onto the bed of the cart where he joined him.

He whispered, "They 'ave found the body of our friend Monsieur Marie and are looking for the assassin. According to my friend on the nag he is a devil with two demons beside him according to the reports."

Marty was facing backwards and looked for Antton. He eventually spotted him after looking past him several times as he had changed out of the police uniform into clothes that made him look more like a gypsy than anything else. What he didn't see was the checkpoint manned by a mix of Chasseurs and infantry soldiers coming up in front of them. The driver alerted Serge, who swore but there was nothing they could do but sit there and try and bluff it out. Marty hoped the driver wouldn't give them up, but a glance at his face as he looked at the soldiers told him that was unlikely.

They sat in line for twenty minutes until it was their carts turn. The driver was questioned by one soldier while another walked around the cart and asked Serge for their papers. He asked Serge some questions and then asked the driver something, who nodded and said, "Certainement, Mon Sargeant."

I bloody wish I knew what was being said, thought Marty. He thought about the note, which was still tucked in his boot, and seemed to be burning a hole in his ankle.

The soldier suddenly thrust his face over the side of the wagon and yelled, "BOO." He had been expecting that as it seemed to be the standard test to see if he was really deaf so didn't look up or react in any way. The man muttered something, stepped back, and waved a hand to the other soldier who also stepped back and waved them through.

Marty stayed absolutely still until they rounded a corner and were out of sight of the checkpoint. Then he turned and looked at Serge with wide eyes and held up his hands in a gesture that could only mean, "How the hell did we get away with that!" Serge smiled and put his finger to his lips and nodded towards the driver, who was keeping up a steady stream of angry commentary and waving his hands around. The horse ignored him and just kept plodding on.

As they passed a gap in the hedge that lined the road and no one else was in sight, Serge suddenly took Marty's arm and urged him off the back off the wagon and through the gap. They spun to the side and hid tight up against the back side of the hedge, letting the cart pull away from them. They could hear the driver's rant fading into the distance. He didn't even know they had left.

They stayed put until the sun went down when they got back on the road and walked until they found a gap on the South side. The moon was in its first quarter and was low on the horizon, so they took that as roughly East and started walking South. They soon saw the outline of some hills in their path and Serge steered to skirt them to the West. They walked over rough terrain with a lot of scrub until just before dawn they came upon a stone quarry. They were both exhausted by now and when they found, what looked like, a disused shed in a corner of the quarry they settled down for the day. They still had some bread and cheese to share, and Marty went out and found some water which he brought back in an old pot that he found discarded behind the shed. He had to plug a hole with a rag and some grass, but it held water long enough.

Marty asked Serge what had been said during the different confrontations.

"The man Antton killed, very professionally I must say, was a member of the Department for internal security. They are responsible for counterintelligence," as Marty looked a little confused, he explained, "They look for spies and traitors who are working with the British. He told me that someone had recognised me at the checkpoint into the town and that I had a poor disguise. He wanted to know if I 'ad bought you, so you were very convincing."

"And the wagon driver?" prompted Marty.

"He was no friend of the revolution, 'e 'ad been a farmer before but whenever the army came by 'is farm they just took what they wanted and didn't pay 'im. They said he should be proud to support the revolution. But you cannot eat pride. Zo 'e left the farm and got work as a driver. 'e suspected we were the ones who had killed the agent but would not turn us in. He wished it 'ad been 'im."

They rested all morning but around mid-afternoon they heard voices outside the hut. Marty found a gap between two boards he could look through. About forty feet away were what looked to be a quarryman and two soldiers. The soldiers were questioning the man who was shaking his head and wringing his woollen hat in his hands. Then one of the soldiers looked over to the hut and asked another question. The quarryman shook his head and shrugged his shoulders. Marty turned to Serge and whispered what was happening.

Luckily, the door to the hut was on the opposite side from the soldiers and the two of them crept out of it and down into some brush about twenty feet behind it. The brush was mainly hawthorn, or the local equivalent and they got some nasty scratches worming their way in.

They lay very still, not even daring to breath heavily as they heard the soldiers search the hut and walk around looking at the scrub prodding it with their bayonets. Now, the thorns were their allies as neither soldier was keen on getting into the thick of them. One of them said something, the other agreed, and they walked back into the quarry.

They waited until it was dark, and carefully wormed their way out of the thicket trying to avoid getting stuck. Once free, they set out in a direction tending Southeast.

It was hard going again as the terrain undulated and they had to detour around villages. After about four hours of walking and clambering they saw the sea. From a piece of high ground, they could see that they were too far East as they could see a pair of islands directly to the South of them, which must be the Isle de Jarre and the Isle Calseraigne. So, they turned West and kept walking.

They reached the inlet after around two miles and spent some time finding a sheltered hidden spot where they could spend the day. Around an hour before dark, they roused themselves and worked their way up to a place where they could look out to sea. Because he was worried about where Antton had got to, Marty scanned inland as well.

He stiffened then reached out, touching Serge on the arm, pointing to the Northeast where he could see a line of black dots moving towards them. They could only be soldiers. They watched them for a few minutes and saw that they had maybe an hour before they would have them sitting in their laps. Marty turned back to the sea and scanned to see if he could make out a boat approaching from the Fortune. Another half hour passed, and he was finding it hard to see the soldiers in the growing dark, even though they were getting uncomfortably close.

Another ten minutes passed, and he was getting very nervous, they were bound to be discovered if the soldiers got much closer and they had nowhere to run as their backs were to the sea. But all they could do was sit and wait.

Darkness was closing in and they heard a shouted command which sounded worryingly close. Then three hundred yards away a torch bloomed into fire followed by others all along the line. Another shouted command and the line started moving forward again. Then he heard a splash and he turned to look out to sea. He couldn't see anything no matter how hard he peered into the night.

A glance over his shoulder showed the line was now a mere two hundred yards away and he decided he wouldn't go without a fight, so he pulled his knives and prepared himself. Then he thought he heard a creak. He listened. There! Definitely a creak. A glance towards the soldiers. Bugger! Less than one hundred yards!

Suddenly, there was a flare of light in the line a hundred yards to the East followed by a series of bangs and a scream. He caught a movement out of the corner of his eye and one of the soldiers nearest to them collapsed to the ground and his torch went out. Then he heard scrabbling and a shape loomed up in front of them. He immediately got to his feet and held his knives at the ready when he heard a familiar voice say quietly, "Hola, Mr. Martin."

"Antton?" he gasped

"Oui, I come plus vitte," said the grinning Antton, and shook the hand of Serge.

Serge looked over his shoulder at something he heard and said, "Ze boat; she is here. Let us go."

Back on board the Fortune, Marty and Serge were in the captain's cabin being debriefed over a hot coffee and a spread of cold meats and cheese. He was grateful for both as he had had nothing to eat or drink since their stop in the quarry. Serge was telling the story of their trip and Marty was not paying too much attention until he mentioned Antton.

Captain Gentry looked at Marty at that point and asked, "Were you aware that Antton Elkano had left the ship and followed you?"

"No sir. I were as surprised as Serge when he popped up behind that secret police bloke. I've no idea how he even got ashore," Marty stated.

"Ah, well I can shed some light on that for you. After the boat returned from dropping you off, he was noted as absent when we took sail. I must admit to having a certain suspicion as your men had practically forced themselves into the boat crew and were overly cheerful and full of themselves when they got back. So, I called Tom Savage in to see me. I told him unless he could come up with a really good reason why Elkano was absent without permission, I would mark him down as run! Well, he was twisting his hat in his hands and told me that he and his mates were worried that you were going ashore with 'that Frenchie'." He inclined his head to Serge, "without anyone from your division to look after you. I told him I hardly thought you needed looking after, but he was unrepentant. So, it turns out they hid Elkano in the boat before it was boarded by the crew and they somehow distracted the cox and got him on shore without being seen. I questioned the cox about it as well and he denies any involvement, although I have my doubt about that as well!" He pauses to sip his coffee.

"So, this time I am going to let Elkano's 'initiative' go without being recorded, but I will not tolerate independent action by any of the crew in future, no matter how good their intentions. Is that clear?"

"Aye, Aye, sir," replied Marty, blushing slightly, embarrassed that his men would take that kind of risk for him.

Serge finished the story and the captain asked if any of this should be put down in a written report to the Admiral.

"Mais Non, mon Capitain," said Serge, "I will send a coded report to my superiors and deliver the message to the admiral myself. I will give 'im a spoken report only."

"Fine," said Captain Gentry, "we will rendezvous again with the Falcon in the next couple of days and pass the admiral's orders to Captain Turner. I am sure he will have a new report for us to take back to Gibraltar by then."

Marty was dismissed and went out on deck where he saw six men standing around by the main mast who, when they saw him, had huge grins on their faces.

"I don't know what you lot be so pleased about cus you be all lucky you ain't in irons." The grins didn't lessen and there wasn't a hint of remorse in any of them.

"I give up, you're all crazy," he said, throwing his hands in the air, then relented and grinned back at them.

Later, when he was lying in his cot listening to the sounds of the Fortune making her way to the rendezvous, he thought about his adventure. His only regret was that he couldn't understand hardly a word that was said.

Well, I can do sommit about that, he thought and resolved to get his French speakers to teach him the language. He also realised that he had really enjoyed the thrill and suspense during his adventure.

"Wouldn't half mind doin' that again," he said to the ceiling.

Epilogue

The rendezvous with the Falcon went smoothly and Captain Turner decided that, for now, Marty would benefit from the added responsibility that came in a smaller ship. The word was that the new First Lieutenant had buckled down and was making a half decent job of it. So, they spent the next three months running back and forth with messages, reports, stores and escorting the odd prize or two. They even got to take a couple themselves.

In October 1794, Hood retired and Hoffam took over from him as the next in line. Marty never found out what was in the message he had carried so far in his boot.

In March of 1795, the Falcon was sent back to England for a refit and Marty was transferred back on board so he could go home as well. He had thoroughly enjoyed his time with Captain Gentry, *but all good things come to an end,* he thought.

When they arrived in Portsmouth in mid-March, Marty had just celebrated his fourteenth birthday and had logged one and a half years at sea. He was taller, a lot taller, and had developed broad shoulders and a confident stance that anyone who had known him before would never recognise. He had kept up his letter writing and now, he had a couple of months of free time before he had to re-join the Falcon after her time at the yard. He intended to visit the de Marchets family in London, but first he would check in on his family and Miss Turner in Dorset.

He took a post chase to Wareham and then, because it was a nice day, he walked to Stoborough across the Causeway to Miss Turner's house. He had left instructions for his sea chest to be sent there from the posting house. He walked up the path and before he had got halfway the door opened, and Emily stood there beaming at him, "My lord, be that you, Marty?" she said, "My, how you've grown! Look at you all dressed up like a gentleman. Miss has read us your letters, but seeing you here, well…"

"Let him in, Emily," Said Katy Turner from the hallway, "you will talk him to death."

Marty put down the duffel he was carrying and stepped up to Emily, gave her a kiss on the cheek, and then turned to Katy. He saw she was worried about something and she asked him to follow him into the parlour.

"I have some news that I need to tell you before you go and visit your mother. I am sorry, but your father passed away just after Christmas. His injuries got the better of him and he didn't want to live on like that. He is buried in Arne church next to your brother."

Marty didn't react, he would save his grief for the graveside but said, "It was probably for the best. He must have hated not being able to care for mum and having to be cared for. Is mum at the house I got her?"

Katy said she was and called for her carriage to be made ready so they could go straight there.

It wasn't far to the house, which was on Furzebrook Road just after the turn off from the Corfe Road, and an easy walk from the village for those whose only mode of transportation was their feet. It was a nice stone cottage with a garden turned over to growing vegetables, but at this time of year was almost empty except for shallots that had been planted in November and the last of the winter greens.

When the coach pulled up, his mother came to the door and for a long moment, she looked at him without really recognising him. But when it dawned on her that this tall handsome stranger in uniform was her little Marty, she rushed forward to sweep him up in her arms, weeping and laughing at the same time. It wasn't long before his brothers and sisters were there as well. He had brought them all presents and handed them out in the parlour. Of course, he had to tell them all about his adventures and had to show his brothers his fighting knife. They were disappointed he didn't have his pistols on him as well, but they were packed in his chest.

The visit was nice, but he realised he had left that life behind him and didn't have much in common with his family anymore. So, it was with a sense of relief and a little guilt that he left to go to London at the end of the week.

He was welcomed by the de Marchets family and they insisted that he stay at their grand house. He surprised them with his mastery of the French language, and they teased him for the Basque accent he had picked up from his men. Evelyn was as pretty as ever and had blossomed into a young woman. He spent as much time with her as he could.

He visited his bank and a prize agent who had been recommended by Crabshaw in Gibraltar. It turned out that he was moderately wealthy even by the measure of the posh folks in London and awash with loot by the measure of a Dorset boy.

While he was in London, he bumped into Serge, who took him to a chop house for lunch so they could catch up. Marty proudly demonstrated his French much to the chagrin of the people on the next table. Serge was impressed and asked him to meet a friend of his and said, "I should tell you my name is actually Armand Clavelle," he laughed and said, "but if you want, I will answer to Serge."

They left the chop house and went to a residence not far from the Admiralty. Armand knocked on the door, and a butler opened it. He immediately gestured them in and once inside, took their coats and hats.

"Mr. Wickham is in the study. Please follow me," he said.

Marty didn't know the name and if he did, he would have probably run like hell, for William Wickham was the spymaster of England.

THANK YOU FOR READING!

I hope you enjoyed reading this book as much as I enjoyed writing it. Reviews are so helpful to authors. I really appreciate all reviews, both positive and negative. If you want to leave one, you can do so on Amazon, Goodreads or my website.

About the Author

Christopher C Tubbs is a dog loving descendent of a long line of Dorset clay miners and has chased his family tree back to the sixteenth century in the Isle of Purbeck. He has been a public speaker at conferences for most of his career in the Aerospace and Automotive industries and was one of the founders of a successful games company back in the 1990's. Now in his sixties he finally got around to writing the story he had been dreaming about for years. Thanks to Inspiration from the great sea authors like Alexander Kent, Dewey Lambdin, Patrick O'Brian and Dudley Pope he was finally able to put digit to keyboard.

You can visit him on his website
www.thedorsetboy.com
Or tweet him @ChristopherCTu3

And   **Now!**

A preview from book two – The Special Operations Flotilla.

Chapter 1 Back to the mast

Martin Stockley, Midshipman on His Majesty's Ship Falcon, a sixth-rate frigate currently completing her refit in Portsmouth, stepped off the Post Chase from London and took a deep breath of sea air. It was late June 1795 and it looked to be shaping up into a pleasant summer. Portsmouth smelled far better than London even with the docks pervading the air with the scent of rotting garbage and other unspeakable things that people thought if they threw it into the water would just disappear. All that happened in reality is all the garbage just washed back and forth on the tide and didn't go anywhere.

He retrieved his sea chest and paid a porter to take it to the George Hotel, where he would stay until he could re-join his ship in a couple of days' time. She was currently having her masts re-stepped and once that was done, he would boat over and take his place back in the cockpit with the other Mids.

His time in London had been spent in the London home of the Count de Marchets and his family, who were refugees from the French Revolution. He had been instrumental in their escape from Toulon just before the city was overrun by the revolutionaries and was treated as a favoured nephew. The Count's daughter, Contessa Evelyn, and Martin were firm friends. He had felt attracted to her in a way that threatened to go beyond friendship as she was becoming a beautiful young woman, but he wasn't ready for that just yet.

He had also run into Armand, a French Navy officer and spy, who he had accompanied on a secret mission in Marseille. He had introduced him to William Wickham who was someone important in the English Security Service. They had talked about his adventures in Marseille and Toulon and talked in French. They had complimented him on his mastery of the language but said he needed to work on his accent as he had a definite Basque twang.

Wickham had asked him what he thought of the experience and he had answered honestly that he had found it exciting but was frustrated he couldn't have been a more active participant. The two men had laughed at that and exchanged a knowing look.

He arrived at the hotel and entered the common room which was full of Naval officers waiting to join ships or looking for a ship to join. He had sent a message ahead to book a room. So, when he arrived, he just announced his arrival to the nearest member of staff, waited to receive his key and arranged for a servant to take his chest to his room.

He was about to go up to it when he was hailed from the bar. His fellow Midshipman Patrick Mulhoon was calling him over to a group of Mids stood at the bar drinking beer. Mulhoon was seventeen years old and one of Martin's best friends on the Falcon.

"Gentlemen" he said in his soft Irish accent "may I introduce Mr Martin (Marty to his friends) Stockley a shipmate on the Falcon and a proper fighting sailor" He grabbed Marty by the arm and drew him into the crowd.

"So, you are the famous 'Marty'" said a tall lad of around eighteen years old with a refined accent who pronounced Marty 'Martee' in a French accent. "James Hepworth, late of the Victory and now of the Frigate Surprise." He introduced himself and held out his hand, which Marty shook as he blushed bright pink.

"We had the pleasure of the Count de Marchets and his delightful daughter on our voyage back from Gibraltar. We were all smitten and trying to woo the beautiful Contessa," he added with a sly wink. Marty bristled but then James continued, "but to no avail as she had already been smitten with her 'hero Martee'. Who had gallantly and singlehandedly rescued the fair maid not once, but twice!" He grinned at Marty who stammered that it wasn't singlehanded and he was sure she exaggerated it all .... really .....

The boys laughed and slapped him on the back. James ordered him a beer and asked him

"What really happened then?"

Marty started telling his version, but Patrick took over saying he was being too modest and gave an exaggerated and extremely blood thirsty account dwelling on the knife and tomahawk killings. After that he had to show them his fighting knife and let them hold it. A young mid from the Circe even managed to cut himself on it much to everyone's amusement.

Later, alone in his room looking out over the harbour with a swimming head from a couple of beers too many, Marty wondered why there were so many Frigates in port at the same time. They were the workhorses of the fleet and there were never enough of them. So why were they here? The papers had been full of the Battle of Genoa where Admiral Hoffam and elements of the Neapolitan fleet had defeated a French fleet capturing two French ships. In his opinion he agreed with Nelson that it was a bit of a nothing battle, and an opportunity had been lost for a much bigger victory.

He woke up with a headache, "serves you right" he said to himself in the mirror as pair of red rimmed, bloodshot eyes looked back at him. He dressed and went down to the common room for breakfast and as he entered, he saw a familiar face at a table by the window. "Hello Richard" he said to Lieutenant Richard Dicky, Fourth Lieutenant of the Falcon, "didn't know you were staying here."

"I'm not" he replied rising and shaking Marty's hand "I'm berthed on board. I came ashore to find you and Mulhoon. Our schedule has been brought forward and the captain wants you onboard. As the breakfast here is one of the best in Portsmouth, I decided to take advantage and get one in. Join me."

They settled down to a large breakfast from a buffet set up on the bar. They filled their plates from a selection of kippers, kidneys, devilled eggs, fried eggs, lamb chops, sausages, mashed potatoes, bacon, bread, butter, honey, jam, marmalade, tea and coffee.

As only young men can, they chowed down and cleared a prodigious amount of food. After about an hour they exchanged belches and Marty asked the hosteler to rouse Mr Mulhoon and to have both of their sea chests brought down as they had to join their ship immediately.

Mulhoon sat beside Marty in the middle of the gig with his head in his hands and groaned. He hadn't had the benefit of a huge calorie laden breakfast or copious amounts of coffee so he was getting the full effect of mixing beer and brandy the night before. Richard Dicky took great delight in steering the boat over the worst of the waves in a way that caused it to rock and pitch to make him feel even worse, but they eventually arrived at the Falcon and jokingly asked him if they needed to get a chair rigged to sling him onboard. Mulhoon manfully stood and climbed the battens up the side to gain the deck, but his misery didn't stop there. The ship was a mass of shouting, hammering, sawing, swearing and worse the smell of paint and tar. It even made Marty wince.

The First Lieutenant, Mr Hill, approached, took one look at Mulhoon and told him to get below and report on deck when he was able to work. He then cast an eye over Marty seeing the bloodshot eyes but noting that he stood erect and wasn't too green around the gills.

"Get into your slops Mr Stockley and take charge of your division. They are helping erect the rigging on the foremast. We want this ship ready to sail in record time." He looked along the deck then back at Marty "Are you still here?" Marty snapped a salute and said, "No Sir" and ran for the ladder down to the cockpit.

His division looked pleased to see him. They had been under the command of a boson's mate who was a meddler. He didn't let them get on with their work, which they all knew how to do but kept stopping them to describe the next step of the operation. Marty asked the mate what the task was and then told him to 'go find something else to do as he would take care of it now' and 'thank you for your efforts.'

He looked at his men and said, "Now will you men get on with raising that cathead up to the top of the mast, or am I going to have to call the steps?"

"We be on it Mr Stockley!" shouted John Smith the fourth (John Smith the third had ruptured himself and had to be put ashore so John had gone from the fifth to the fourth now).

The ships fiddler was grinding out 'Jack's the Lad' from atop the capstan and the men picked up the beat to coordinate the heave. From then on, the work went easy. Marty told them what he wanted doing and they did it, unless of course none of them had done it before and then they would talk it over with Marty or he would consult with a mate or another officer if necessary. Marty watched and learned. He didn't assume he knew better than the men just because he had a higher rank.

A week of hard work saw them ready to bring the guns aboard. The Falcon's hull had been strengthened with new Knees and re-enforcements to the gun deck and was being rearmed with twenty-six new eighteen pounders rather than the twenty-eight nine pounders she had before. They were also fitting long nine's as bow chasers and four six pounders on the quarterdeck making her up to a thirty-two-gun ship. That of course didn't include the six thirty-two-pound carronades, two at the bow on the fore deck and four on the quarterdeck that gave her an awesome close in punch. Marty made sure his beloved carronades were installed correctly and that their gun crews took personal responsibility for their installation. The Falcon now had one hell of a punch and a full two hundred and fifty-man crew.

In the evenings when the work stopped, Marty found Roland du Demaine, engaged him in conversation and he in turn pulled in the other Frenchmen. They talked, Marty's vocabulary increased, and he learnt to speak with not only a Parisian accent but the one from Lyon as well. Quite accidently he also absorbed information about the hometowns of the three Frenchmen and lots of little facts about the way of life in France.

After all the guns were installed, they started provisioning the ship. The First Lieutenant and the Captain were carefully planning the location of the stores so that not only was the ship trimmed perfectly when she was fully laden but as the stores were used the trim would be maintained. Marty oversaw the stores coming onboard and kept a record of what and how many that would be passed to Mr Evans the Purser.

The Falcon was lucky they had that rare bird that was an honest purser who was actually liked by the crew. He was making a fair profit, but he didn't rob them blind or cheat them in the process. When the salt beef and pork was delivered Evans inspected the dates and condition of every one of the casks. He rejected out of hand a complete delivery where the casks were dated 1767. He wasn't having nearly thirty-year-old salt beef on his ship! That caused a visit from the provisioning officer who came prepared to read the riot act to Evans but for some reason walked away without saying a word when Evans said something quietly in his ear just after he boarded. Marty strongly suspected Evans knew something the Provisioning Officer didn't want made public.

Next came the water hoys and the taking on of tons of fresh water stored in casks that were brand new and had been commissioned by the captain at his own cost. Personal stores and livestock came onboard last.

They warped the ship out of the dock and towed her over to the powder dock. This was the most dangerous part of the whole provisioning as they hoisted a full load of powder down into the magazine. No naked flames, absolutely no smoking and all metal objects that could cause sparks, put away. The deck was sanded and wetted to catch any stray powder grains that may have leaked and thoroughly washed down afterwards.

After that they went for a short shakedown cruise to check that nothing fell off or broke and that everything worked as it was supposed to. They even fired off the guns to check the tackles worked just so. When they returned to Portsmouth Captain Turner reported them ready for sea in all respects.

Typically, they heard nothing for almost a week.

Books by Christopher C Tubbs

The Dorset Boy Series.

A Talent for Trouble

The Special Operations Flotilla

Agent Provocateur

In Dangerous Company

The Tempest

Vendetta

The Trojan Horse

La Licorne

Raider

Silverthorn

Exile

The Scarlet Fox Series

Scarlett

A Kind of Freedom

Legacy

The Charlamagne Griffon Chronicles

Buddhas Fist

Website: www.thedorsetboy.com
Twitter: @ChristoherCTu3
Facebook: https://www.facebook.com/thedorsetboy/
YouTube: https://youtu.be/KCBR4ITqDi4

Published in E-Book, Paperback and Audio formats on Amazon, Audible and iTunes